OUTSIDE WESTON LIBRARY

OUTSIDE WESTON LIBRARY

A NOVEL

ONYEKA NWELUE

NEW YORK & LONDON

First published in Great Britain in 2022 by
Abibiman Publishing

First published in India in 2022 by
Abibiman Publishing India
www.abibimanpublishing.com

Published in the United Kingdom by Abibiman Publishing,
an imprint of Abibiman Music & Publishing, London.

Abibiman Publishing is registered under
Hudics LLC in the United States and in the United Kingdom.

ISBN: 9781739693428

Cover design by Gabriel Ogunbade
Illustrations by Anwuacha Frank Achulike
Cover photo: Onyeka Nwelue

Printed by Clays Ltd.

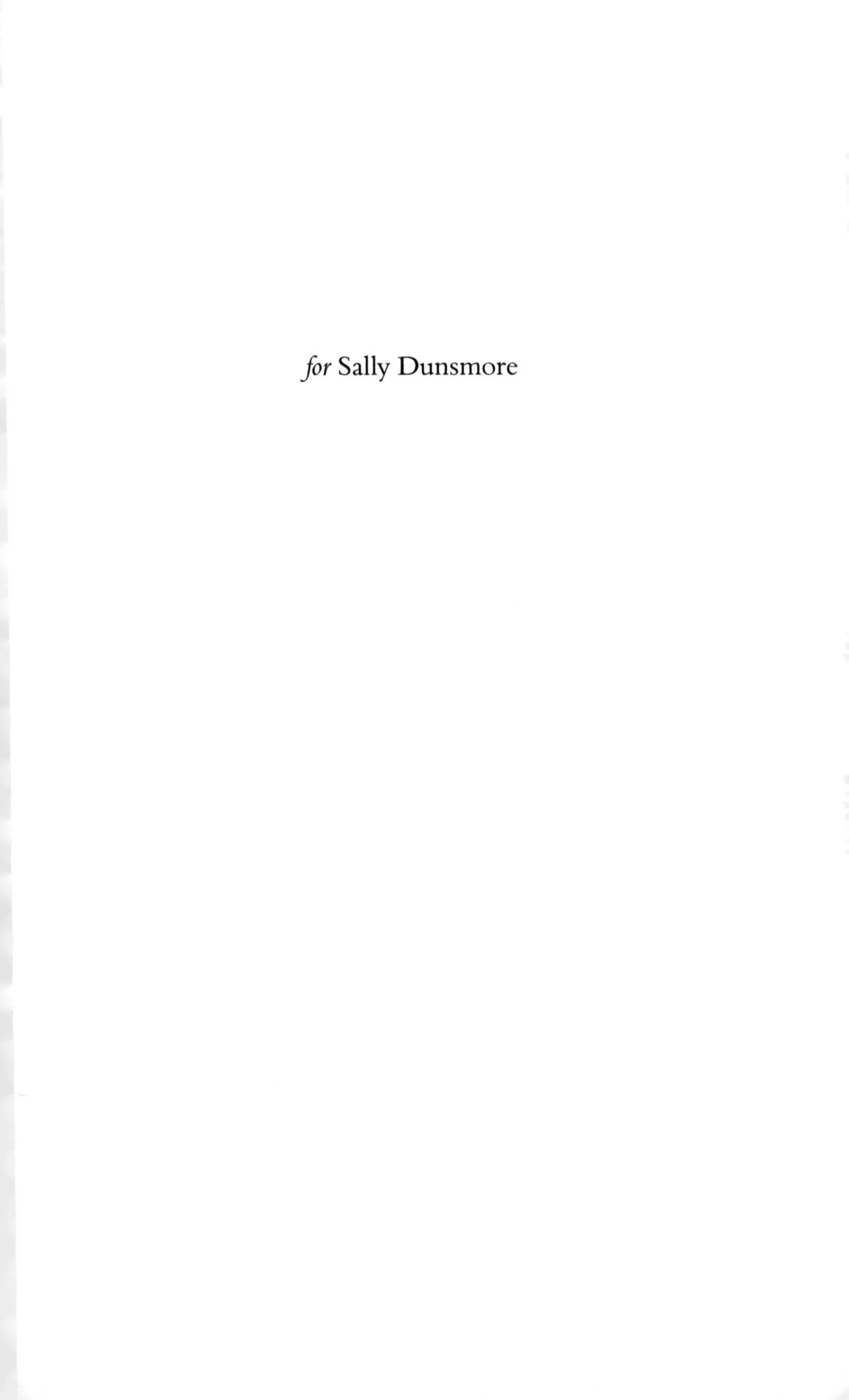

for Sally Dunsmore

I wasn't Nigerian because he had assumed upon sighting me that I was Igbo.

It took him a little while to learn about Haiti and to come to terms with the fact that Haitians are mostly Igbo people who had been brought across the Atlantic, and over time had organized and overthrown the French and declared themselves a republic.

And he was surprised to learn of how much I knew of the Nigerian contemporary music culture, food, Nollywood and attitude. I showed him the number of Nigerian celebrities I followed on Instagram.

When I told him that we bought CDs of Nollywood movies in Haiti, he nearly would have disbelieved me. To assuage his doubts, I told him about Genevieve Nnaji, Ramsey Noah, Omotola Jalade Ekeinde, Jim Iyke, and Zuby Michael.

The things I told him about Nigeria made him become apologetic that he knew nothing about my country, and so he had put in effort to learn as much as he could about me in the shortest time possible.

Michael, I would later learn, was from a rich home.

And although he had lived much of his early life in the United States, a family feud had made his father relocate to Nigeria with the rest of the family.

Michael told me that he had hated the idea at first but had soon come to love Nigeria more than he could possibly have loved anywhere else. He told me that

Nigeria was the best place one could possibly live as long as one had money and wasn't beset by the social shortcomings that Nigeria had come to be reputed for. And truly, he had lived a life insulated from hardships.

His father's business ventures, and political connections saw to it, and soon he divorced himself from every idea of returning to the United States as he had earlier nursed. It was with reluctance, he told me, that he had accepted his father's decision to ship him off to Oxford to get an elitist education, and the most important in the world. It was not his dream, but his father's and he would only give the old man the satisfaction that he craved for the length of time that it demanded, after which he would reclaim his life and live it as he chose.

"What would you want to do after studies?" I had asked Michael one day.

"I will become a musician."

"Like Davido?"

"Yes, and no," he had replied with a dismissive air which, to my perception, indicated his displeasure at being compared to anyone.

"Why *no*? I am interested in that part."

"I will do things differently."

"How exactly?"

"I don't know. But I will."

"Will you be doing hip-hop?"

His eyes lit up with excitement. "Of course, my

brother. Hip-hop is the real thing. I mash up the whole place with it, promote myself to the end of the world and make sure to bring home a Grammy, for the culture."

"Will your father approve of your being a musician?"

"Well," he said with a shrug that showed the dampness that had come over his spirits. "My old man will have to deal with it. I can't live in his shadows."

"I learned that Davido's father wasn't pleased with his decision to be a musician either."

"Yes, you know how it is with these men. They think that they know it all. Music is as important as anything, and a musician can become as important as a president too. Don't you have Wyclef Jean in Haiti? He is more famous than your President. What is his name again?"

"Jovenel Moise."

"Yes, President Moise. I remember now. You see my point now? I remember your music star more than I do your president."

"Wyclef ran for president at some point."

"Yes, I remember. That was after he did a fundraising for Haiti, following the earthquake. I read the news in Times magazine. I was hoping Wyclef would win. I love that guy. I remember listening to *Diallo.* Everyone in Nigeria knows that song. They can sing it by heart. Some years later I listened to someone tell me the story of Diallo the immigrant who was killed by the police in the United States."

Michael talked a lot about being a musician that at

some point I began to believe in his dream for the sheer reason of repetition than for seeing his commitment to it. He played no instruments and I have never seen him practise writing songs. His relationship to music, apart from his penchant for talking about it and everything else that happened with artists' lives, was in singing along to music whenever he played songs in his room or on his headphones. In between music, he would stop to tell me how Ice Prince bought the latest Benz and how it was said that another artist was having a row with a South African counterpart.

TWO

Tou manti pa fon

Back in Haiti, my grandmother would say, "The hole of lies isn't deep." This means that you don't have to look far for the truth to be revealed.

So, I always think of Haiti with a longing.

In my exciting preparations to get to Oxford I had never made any room for coping with the moment when I would think of home.

It never did strike me that, in Oxford, I would have to contend with the emotion.

My homesickness had a form—*Jesula*. The daughter of a businessman who struggled to get a footing in the mining business.

We had been classmates in school, from our earliest school years. And then we had gone on to secondary school together and found ourselves always being at the same place, including attending the same churches, that for a while I began to think that our fates were similar.

Jesula.

She was only a year younger. Slim, with skin the colour of chocolate. And her hair was always low-cropped and permed.

We kissed in the back of the classroom block.

Of course we didn't tell anyone. I am sure none of her friends knew. I didn't have many friends and the few that I had were never to know that I had gotten my first kiss. A year later, she gave me a taste of it at the shed in her family's bungalow where I had snuck in one evening when no one was at home. It was not her first time, she said. Although there was no way I could tell. She was the one who told me that she was supposed to bleed were it the first time. I was glad that she didn't. Why would I be the one to make Jesula bleed? I asked her if she bled the first time, and she nodded. I asked her who did it. She told me to forget it. It was as though she knew that at that point I was nursing a desire to kill whomever it was.

We made out more often when we had the chance. Three years later, after we had had a quarrel spurred on by her suspicion that I was having a thing with her elder sister, she went off to France with the rest of her family where her father had just gotten appointed at the Ministry of Foreign Affairs.

It broke my heart, and I am sure it broke hers too.

We had successfully kept things from public notice, or so I thought, until one day my father came home looking all angry.

I was summoned to his room later that night and I stood stupefied when he asked to verify if it was true what he heard that day about Jesula and me.

My prolonged silence must have irritated him for he screamed his displeasure at me, so loud that it brought every occupant of the house rushing to his room to know what the fracas was.

"This rascal will put all of us in trouble one day!" my father boomed, pointing an accusing finger at me, and that was all he said that night before ordering everyone, including myself, to leave his room.

It was the first time I had seen myself become a victim of my father's periodic sour mood which was often noticed when he had a bad day at the ministry. In those times, he would be recluse and would only raise his voice at anyone or anything who stood in his way, and it was often always my mother, and she had learned to cope with it by totally ignoring him, and when his mood became better, he would apologize for his behaviour towards her or anybody he had directed his frustrations at.

In my case, my father never apologized, but it was

from my mother that I was to learn that Jesula's father was standing in the way of the approval of my father's proposal for an irrigation project at the Ministry of Agriculture. He was to gather from a close source that Jesula's father held grudges against my father because *his son* had *let loose his wantonness on his innocent daughters.*

Truth is that I have never had a thing with Jesula's elder sister, at least not as Jesula suspected.

Lovelie - that was her name. Slender like her sister, she had a much lighter skin colour because she had been the outcome of a romantic affair which her father had when he had gone for a diplomatic mission. They said that three years later Lovelie's mother had died and so the little girl had been reunited with her father and brought into his household.

Different versions existed of how livid Jesula's mother had been and the issues that attended the reunion, but Lovelie had remained with the family, and it was clear to all who bothered to know that she had come to stay.

In the rare moments that I passed Lovelie on the road, we never so much as exchanged a glance or a word in greeting. It wasn't for any reason that this was so, but we had nothing in common. I was sure she knew nothing about what I had with her sister, Jesula.

Maybe this would have formed a common ground of familiarity between us, but because she apparently didn't know this, and, as I suspected, Jesula had very well concealed our clandestine affair, I saw no need to exchange any glances or words in greeting with Lovelie whenever we passed each other. But this was to change one day when I looked up from a book I was reading one evening in a football field to find Lovelie hovering over me.

"What's that book you are reading?" she asked.

Her voice left me stupefied for a moment. It was the first time I was hearing it, and I was not prepared for it. Because I couldn't find my tongue, I turned the book over so that she could see the title. *Madame Bovary, she* mouthed. "Is it yours?"

"Yes," I finally brought myself to say.

"Could I borrow it when it is done?"

"Yes … Sure … I will be done tomorrow."

On the next day, Lovelie met me after school and asked if I was done with reading the book. I had it ready for her and handed it over. She treated me to a most charming smile and promised to handle the book with care and return it to me when she was done. It was that exchange that Jesula had seen and made her conclusions. But truth be told, that smile that Lovelie gave me was more satisfying than anything that Jesula could possibly give, and I would do anything to have that smile given to me repeatedly.

Yet I was certain that Jesula was more preferable. She was safe for me, nothing like the consuming beauty that was Lovelie, so beautiful that I would have to constantly fight off other people who would want her. But I am sure Jesula never knew this, that she was the one I would choose any day over Lovelie; she was more dependable, a surer footing for me.

After her family moved to the capital, I didn't hear from Jesula for many months. I had actually begun to forget about her until one morning I got a message from her. She had written me from Port-au-Prince.

There was nothing serious about the letter. It was at least what I suspected, so I didn't treat the messenger who delivered the letter with any seriousness, especially when I recognized the handwriting on the envelope.

In the letter, Jesula had wanted to know how I was doing and how the town was faring in her absence. There was nothing personal about the way she asked about trifle issues and closed the letter with warm wishes to me. I tore up the letter afterwards, deposited the pieces in a wastebin outside our bungalow and forgot all about the letter and Jesula.

Five days later, another letter arrived. It was also from Jesula. Yet again, I didn't pay it any serious attention. Like the one before it, it was a letter that conveyed no serious emotion. In it, Jesula had enquired as to how I was faring, and hinted as to how things were going with her family in their new home and the difficulty in making new friends. It was a big house they lived in. She told me and that her father was not always at home. Yet again she had closed it with kindest regards to me.

Two more letters afterwards, she apologized for her accusation; according to her letter, she had talked things over with her sister and had realize that nothing of the sort which she accused me of was at play between her sister and me.

Her suspicions were unfounded, she confessed, and borne out of a feeling of insecurity. She begged for my forgiveness in the expressed hope that we could patch things up. She missed me, and she told me.

At that moment, I remember that everything she had said didn't mean much to me and it took the next letter to convince me that she meant all that she had told me. It was as though there was some premonition to all of this, for three months later, Jesula's father was returned from his post, an embittered man. But for Jesula and me, it was a good thing. And Lovelie began to pay me some clandestine visits during that time.

THREE

Sa ou fè se li ou wè

This saying, what you do, is what you see, always cracks me up. It simply means what we see in our life, is the result of our actions.

This takes me back to Michael.

"I met this babe," Michael was saying. "If you see this girl, *eh,* you will know that I am being modest in however way I will describe her to you."

We were at Westgate, checking out some shoes in one of the shops where designer brands are sold. I had been reluctant at first to come along with Michael, but by the time he had followed me to my place so I could dispose of my bag, it became clear to me that there was no way I could shake him off or make him buy into my reluctance.

"When did you meet her?"

"Last night."

"Where was I last night?" I asked, wracking my head in an effort to recall where I had been as not to have borne witness to this meeting that sounded so pivotal to my Nigerian friend's existence.

"You were not with me, that is for sure," he said. "You were studying because you want to be the next Chike Obi."

"Chike Obi?"

"Yes. A foremost Nigerian mathematician. Very famous. Everyone back home knows him."

"I would like to meet this dude."

Michael regarded me with an air of amusement, the ridiculousness of which appeared to have no end in sight. It must have been my questioning look that made him snap out of his theatrics.

"The man is dead. Died a long time ago. I can't remember when. But I would wager that he died long before you were born."

"Oh," was I all I could say.

"Will you be free tonight?"

"That depends. Why do you ask?"

"Will you be free or not?" he asked, and settled on a seat in front of a mirror to try out a shoe.

"What do you have in mind?"

"We will go see the babe. The one I was telling you about. Annabelle. She is

Dutch."

"Hmmm."

"She is beautiful."

"Does she meet your usual spec?" I asked.

"Come on, man. Of course, she has nyash. That is the minimum requirement."

Michael's comment elicited from me a burst of laughter and drew some glances our way. If Michael noticed the glances, he didn't care. Instead, he joined me, and laughed to his heart's content. "Yes," he said when he had overcome the spell of laughter. "You don't have to be uptight about it. I like nyash and I am not denying it."

"You are unbelievable, my friend."

"Yes, man. That is how it is. You should come along with me tonight. Annabelle is bringing some friends along. You could hook up with one, you know," he said with a wink.

"I … Tonight I will …"

"Please don't make me begin to think that you are growing antisocial by the day. It is settled. You are coming along. There will still be enough time for you to do all the reading you need to do." Getting up, he asked: "How do these shoes look on me?"

It was a pair of Marks and Spencer shoes. Brown-coloured. I would have preferred boots and not the low top shoes that Michael had a penchant for.

"What will you wear it with?"

"Regular woolen trousers," he said. I contemplated Michael's appearance in the said trousers and shoes. " … with a white shirt."

"I think it will do just fine."

"That's my man," he said with relish, snapping his finger at me. "So, what are you picking?"

"I bought two pairs of shoes only yesterday. Surely, I will find something in my wardrobe that suits."

Annabelle, when I eventually met her that night, was almost everything that Michael had conjured in my head. She wore her luscious hair long and slightly kinky. A likeable girl she was, and her constant smile revealed a set of bad teeth that Michael hadn't prepared me for. It was the only blemish that I could see about her. Perhaps Michael had intentionally left out that part about her. For expediency, perhaps. I couldn't tell. Although he was right about her hips, the one part about her which he didn't make up. It was never in him to make anything up, actually.

We met at a pub where Anabelle, in the company of two other ladies - friends of hers - had apparently downed a first round of beers and were onto their second. They were in a jolly good mood, chatting excitedly at a corner of the pub. She stood up upon spotting us approach their table and, for a moment, I thought she would hug Michael. But she offered him her hands, and he accepted. With a sweeping gesture of her arm she introduced us to her friends, Josy and Suzy. Josy had full bosoms that I could tell would give great concern to her choice of clothing, and her smile was generous. She looked very much like the kind of girl who was conscious of being in a pleasant company. I liked her smile almost immediately. Suzy was a direct opposite as far as phenotypical expressions went, but she was equally cheerful, although a little more reserved. A bit too much of eye-lining made the white of her eyes prominent, and I could tell that she was Middle-eastern.

Michael sat next to Anabelle and her two companions made way for me to lodge myself between them. We ordered for fresh round of beers and took over whatever conversations the girls had been having prior to our arrival. While Michael had Annabelle to himself I was torn between Josy and Suzy and as time went on it became evident that I would gravitate towards Suzy.

A TV screen projected on the wall to one corner of the pub showed a football match, and now and then Michael turned around to check the scores. It was an English team playing. One of the things I had learned quickly about Michael was his interest in football, especially European leagues. He was a Chelsea FC fan and, on countless occasions, had travelled to London to watch the team play. Surprisingly, he didn't care about football leagues in Africa and was a supporter of none of the clubs. I have never been much of a football enthusiast. I only played when I could. Back home we would organise ourselves into a team, one neighbourhood against the other. There had been a competition once, a sort of a league with a prize to be won, but my neighbourhood didn't get any close to the quarter finals. Meeting Michael made me look up football clubs in Africa; I feared that there were none in existence, but then my search had turned up quite a number of football clubs spanning across the continent.

"So, you are from Haiti?"

"Yes," I said, looking to Suzy from whom the answer had come even as she regarded me with unmasked interest.

"Is it close to your friend's country?" she asked, gesturing with a movement of her eyes at Michael.

"Haiti is in the Caribbean."

"Oh, really? Close to Rihanna's country. What's the name again?"

"Trinidad," Josy chipped in. "They say it is such a touristy place."

"She's from Barbados, dimwits!" Anabelle cut in, laughing as she playfully slapped her friends in the arm. Everyone burst out laughing.

"I have a way of mixing up all the countries in the Caribbean," Josy defended.

"My bad."

"I am also guilty of that too," Michael added. "But I will never go wrong with Jamaica. Can't mix that place up with anywhere in the world."

Anabelle smiled. "Of course. You will never go wrong with Jamaica. And I think I know why."

All the girls smiled, exchanging knowing looks.

"Do I have a feeling that you girls are making inferences to ganja?"

"Oh yeah," Anabelle said, leaning into him.

We had some more beers and talked until it was 10 P.M. when the management notified us that it was time to close.

"They think we have access to drugs and that we deal with drugs somehow,"

Michael told me when we were walking home after seeing the girls off to their house.

"You think so?"

"Yea. I know so."

"If they suspect that we are drug dealers, shouldn't it be a reason for them to distance themselves from us?"

Michael nodded knowingly. It was something he does at moments like this, and it leaves me wondering whether he was considering my point or thinking about how to simplify his thought for me to understand. It felt condescending some of the times, but I was getting used to it knowing that he never meant any disrespect.

"Maybe you don't know these girls as I know them,"

he finally said. "Most of them get close to an African because they believe that every African has access to drugs."

"You mean these girls use drugs?" I asked, lowering my voice. We were already within St Anne's College and didn't want to run the risk of being overheard.

"I can bet that they use drugs on occasion. A lot of them are. They experiment with a lot of things - sex, drugs, alcohol, everything."

"You have a point," I said pensively, sticking my hand into my pocket against the cold.

"Now that they know that you are Caribbean, their expectation of getting some marijuana from you has heightened."

"But that is some serious case of racial profiling," I said. "Does the police think the same of me - I mean, us?"

Michael shrugged. "I wouldn't know. It always takes some event for us to find out."

"So what happens when the girls don't get any drugs from us?"

"They will be most disappointed."

"And what happens next?"

"What do you expect to happen next?"

"I don't know. That is why I ask."

"You will have to chill, mate," Michael said, switching over to his exuberant self. "We are just having fun with them ladies. While the going is good, you hit the honey pot as many times as you can so that by the time things go sour, you just move on without looking back."

"That's some way to look at it."

"Yea, bro. That's keeping it real. You know what I mean."

FOUR

Moun ki ba ou konsèy achte kabrit nan lapli, se pa li ki ede w pran swen li nan lesèk

Annabelle and her friends shared a three-bedroom flat tucked away in a side street ten minutes away from campus and a good walk away from the pub where we all met two days later.

We always say, people who advise you to buy goats during the rain, are not the ones who will help you feed them during the drought.

My grandmother explained that people around you

may give you advice, but you are still solely responsible for your actions.

It was the usual drinks and discussions, and there were a lot to talk about so that, again, we were asked to leave when time came for the pub to close for the night. We bought packs of beer at a convenience store, and just as Michael had hinted earlier on, we all headed to their apartment.

It was a spacious house, and an old one. I could tell that there was a basement, even though there was no other way of knowing other than that the floorboards beneath the carpeting creaked in a few spots. Anabelle got us some snacks, and seated on the sitting room floor, paying no attention to the Netflix movie playing on the TV, we drank, chatted and laughed freely.

Almost all of the beer had been spent, even though the ladies had brought out some more from the fridge, when Anabelle and Michael retired to her room, leaving me with the two other girls.

"I will go take a quick shower," Suzy announced.

"Me too," Josy added.

Left alone to myself, in the midst of empty beer bottles that made me appear like a culprit that had been strung up to bear alone the consequences of a communal crime, I focused my attention on the TV screen only to realise how drunk I was.

My focus was a mess, and I was having a hard time making sense of anything that was being displayed on the screen. Giggles and other evidence of excited activity reached me from the bathroom.

My thought went to Michael and whatever it was he must be occupying himself with behind closed doors in the company of his girl - and I dared to call Anabelle that: Michael's girl.

At last Josy and Suzy came out of the bathroom, both in their bathrobes. They joined me in the sitting room. How I fought to keep from staring at the elaborate parting of their bathrobes. Suzy's drew my attention as much as the bountifulness that was Josy's. In my drink addled mind, I knew that I was losing out on the battle of self-control, so I gave myself up to fate when the ladies came over to me.

In my home in Haiti, we were strict Pentecostal Christians.

But, we also practiced Vadou.

For us, it was normal to practice Voodoo, as you folks call it.

Pentecostal Christian.

At least that was what my mother pretended she was.

It was inconceivable to imagine a Sunday when she wouldn't be in church early enough and was one of the last people to leave after consulting with the pastor; a balding man in his forties who carried himself with the swagger of God's head boy. As for my father, I am not sure if he believed in anything remotely religious.

Yet he believed in God for he always prayed before meals.

That was about the only evidence of piety that could be attributed to the man. But for my mother, it was entirely different. She made us wake up every morning, and then she would have the household congregate in the sitting room where we would sing and clap and then she would read from the Bible and interpret from her passage how God who lived beyond the clouds was a disciplinarian who didn't take lightly to any form of sinful disobedience, including disobeying one's parents. And while she was delivering her sermon, no one dared doze off as she saw no wrong in dealing the sleepy head a slap in the midst of her sermons. Whenever we gathered like this, my father never bothered. He would go about his business in the house, getting ready for the day's work.

My mother's most used verse was from the book of Proverbs. While pointing out to us the need to hold onto our family values, she would say "evil communication corrupts good manners." Oh, and there was never forgetting the many times she used that quote, emphasizing it in moments of admonition as in moments of chastisement.

Evil communication corrupts good manners.

I remember that there was a time when it had been discovered that my sister was going out with a boy.

My mother was practically mortified.

She appeared unable to come to terms with the fact that my sister was already having carnal knowledge of a man.

That day, I heard so much that I was not prepared to hear; so much about how my mother had retained her virginity despite material enticement from men whom she mentioned to my sister and to all of us; men whom we saw on TV and some who lived in the same neighbourhood as us.

It was not until she was married to my father, she said to the benefit of our hearing, did she consent to sexual commitments.

Oh, it didn't stop at that. She narrated how she had fled the marital bed on the first night and that my father, worried, had scouted the neighbourhood all night long looking for her until she was found in the market square all by herself, and in shock at the sight of my father's phallus and what he had intended to do with it.

I had never known my mother to be that graphic in such details as that, but that day I was seeing a new bit of her. It appeared that the events of that day had tipped her balance, upsetting something inside of her that she had kept bottled up for too long. And with the way she went about it, one would think that she regretted losing her virginity and would gladly exchange all of us for the opportunity to have it back. Perhaps she had consented to marriage out of pressure from her family.

Father had a good job, and everyone would have called her a fool to have passed off the opportunity to make better her prospects in life when my father had come asking her hand in marriage. I hated to think of it, yet looking back I would not be surprised if she after years of marriage she had grown to abstain from her marital obligations and my father, being the man he was, would have adjusted were necessary to accommodate her wishes.

Typical of my mother, she had blamed my sister's frivolity on the friends she kept.

"Evil communication corrupts good manners," she had stressed for the umpteenth time.

There and then she had declared my sister grounded until further notice. In the meantime, she was to sever every communication with her friends.

In fact, mother had insisted she would have no friends going forward. As though that was not enough, she extended the penalty to the rest of us. No friends, no friends. But why? Because evil communications corrupt good manners.

We were to conduct ourselves, at school, and in the neighbourhood as loners and it should never to be heard that we kept any friends. After all, she didn't keep any friends, she insisted, and her life was peaceful and better off for it.

Therefore, we should learn to stay away from friends, to keep to ourselves, to maintain our chastity, for the God we served was a God who didn't take lightly to sinful conducts of any kind, and while she lived, it remained her obligation to see to it that we were brought up right, in the way of the Lord.

"So, how did you manage it?" Michael asked me the next morning. We were at a cafe having breakfast. There was an unmistakable eagerness about him, urging me to not leave out any detail.

"It happened," I said with a shrug.

"Oh, come on. Don't give me that. I need details."

"What?!" I asked, shoveling a spoon of mashed potatoes into my mouth.

"You just had a three …"

"Shhh … Keep it low."

"You just had a threesome," he continued in a whisper, leaning towards me from across the table. "A threesome, my man, and you are sounding like it's no big deal. Does every man in your country have a harem? You tell me."

"No. Every man in Haiti doesn't have a harem. We are like every other …"

"Forget that one. Concentrate on giving me the answers I need. Don't bother about Haiti, I know much already about there."

"So what do you want to know?"

"How was the experience last night?"

"I had fun," I said reluctantly.

Michael slapped my arm. "Bad guy! Baaad guy! The baddest guy! I knew it that you had it in you. All the while you were just acting up. I came into the sitting room to check on you and I saw all of you spent on the couch."

"You did?"

"Yea, man. And when I saw you, I said to myself, *Yea, man, this is how it ought to be.*"

I laughed in spite of myself. "You are crazy, bro."

"No, man. I am being real. There, you looked like royalty, passed out as you were with more than one woman. I wish I had taken a picture of you."

I nearly choked on my drink of mango juice. "Jeez! You would have taken a picture of us?"

"Yea."

"Thank God it never crossed your mind."

"You have something against pictures? Or are you concerned that I would do post it online or show it around?"

"Well, I meant to say that it could get into the wrong hands, and you know what that means."

"Stop talking shit," Michael said dismissively. "Guzzle up your food, man. I have to be in class in a few minutes."

FIVE

Fòse moun fè sa yo pa vle fè se tankou eseye plen lanmè ak wòch

I was watching Al-Jazeera at ten in the morning.

Outside, Oxford was warming up to a day that didn't hold much promise by way of sunshine and warmth.

Wrapped up on the couch and with a mug of tea handy, I felt I could weather the day quite alright.

On the TV, the French President was giving a speech on climate change.

He was addressing fellow European governments and their representatives in Brussels, I thought.

This is everything politicians do - *talk*.

It is the same all over, whether in my country or in France. They talk and there is not much that comes of it.

Maybe I am wrong.

Actually there are things that come out of it because when I think of it, it becomes clear that politicians put in so much effort into ensuring that nothing actually changes, and that the world remains as it is.

Turning down the volume of the TV, I put on my headphones to listen to Wyclef Jean and to think of my country and the hopes of immigrants like myself and Wyclef. But I still can't keep my mind off the French. Maybe for once the President should tell his audience that his nation is to apologize for the fate of Haiti. Maybe they should begin to talk about doing things right. Only recently it was in the news that to cut carbon emissions, attention should be diverted to rural Africa where the majority cook over log fires. The dishonesty of it!

Forcing people to do what they do not want to do, is like trying to fill the ocean with rocks.

Because I had my headphones on, I didn't hear the repeated knock on my door until my phone rang. It was Michael.

"What's up, man?" he asked when I opened the door. "For a moment, I thought you had smuggled some chic into your crib."

I laughed at the insinuation, wishing that it were

true. “Sorry, I had my headphones on. Didn’t hear you knock.”

He brushed past me into my room and headed straight for the fridge. Returning with a pack of fruit juice, he settled in front of the TV.

“Isn’t that the French President?”

“Yes.”

“You understand French, right? What is he saying?”

“Climate change nonsense. You know them. They always talk. Boring stuff that means nothing and amounts to nothing.”

“The climate change issue is a serious one, you know?”

“I agree. But you know how these people would politicise everything for the sake of economics. There are always the interest of multinational companies which governments have to look out for. I mean, that is why they have lobbyists and a lot of gangsters in corporate attires to twist every agenda for economic and geo-political benefits.”

“You sure know so much for a guy who keeps to himself most of the time. Where do you know all of these things?”

“My father works in government, and I read a lot.”

“Interesting. And I agree you have a point.”

“You know my country has been bearing the brunt of these economic and geopolitical chess games for decades. So we can't afford to be ignorant of these things."

"Sorry, if I ask this, but I thought Haiti has always been poor. What role did foreign governments play in this?"

I laughed. "I know it is an ignorant question. You can just forget I asked it."

"No, no hard feelings. Nigeria and Congo aren't the only African countries with in-demand minerals under its grounds. Haiti is also rich in underground minerals."

"Such as?"

"Gold, natural gas, copper … name it."

"Same shit everywhere," Michael said, shaking his head. "Wherever natural resources are found amongst Africans, the people suffer rather than get enriched."

"That is one part of it. In 1804 Haiti declared herself a republic and liberated herself from the French rule. The French slave owners, unable to bear the humiliation of being kicked out of Haiti by mere slaves, surrounded the island with an armada of warships, and were prepared to bomb everything to smithereens if we didn't pay for *their loss in property* - in this case, slaves. And the fine was a steep one. Twenty billion dollars by today's estimate. We only finished paying the debt in 1947."

"Wow. That is gangster. I never heard of this."

"Do you continental Africans know anything about us?"

Michael shrugged. "Yea, we know a lot about you

guys. You folks in the Caribbean smoke ganja, party on the beach and live a stress-free life. That is why you produce people like Bob Marley, Rihanna, Beyonce, Sean Paul, Shaggy."

"For real? Man!"

"Never mind," he laughed. "I was only pulling your legs."

"So what do you guys on the continent know about us in the diaspora?"

Michael scratched his head. I could see that he was struggling. "Is this an interview?" he asked.

"Something like that."

"Well, for now, I don't know much."

"But you know that we were mostly slaves shipped off through the Atlantic from West Africa?"

He nodded. "Sure that is general knowledge."

"And are you aware that a lot of us in the Caribbean are taught to believe that we are the true sons of Africa, and you, the bastard sons sold us off to the European slave traders so that you could get us out of the way?"

"Wooh wooh! That's big. Where did that come from?"

"But there are proofs, man. For instance, you guys on the continent never care about us. While we are grunting under the heels of imperialist powers, you guys cozy up to them, giving them oil and mineral concessions without negotiating terms that put our plight into consideration."

"Come on, man. This is getting too much …"

"Haiti, the first African Republic has requested a number of times to become a member of the African Union, but each time they are treated as outsiders."

"Yes, I see it makes sense that every diaspora African country should become a member of the African Union. But then it doesn't prove anything about us being the illegitimate sons and therefore ousting you guys."

"If you are the legitimate sons of the continent, how come with all its wealth you have not done anything for yourselves other than dish it out to Europeans and fight amongst yourselves who would become the choicest puppet of European imperialism? From where we stand, yours is a tussle between house niggers for the master's love."

"I think I have had enough of this," Michael said, getting up and heading out. Suddenly remembering the pack of orange juice in his grip, he let it down on my table and banged the door a little too loudly. I didn't care to stop him, even though I thought it was the right thing to do. I had not set out to upset him, but it had happened that way and I had no apologies to make.

Turning off the TV, I went in search of my gym kit. At that point it will serve me better to burn off the frustration lifting weights.

As anyone would expect, things had gone sour between Michael and me. But that was not Michael. He didn't sulk for long. Later that evening, he was at my place again as though nothing happened. Somehow it felt unnatural to me to pretend as though that morning never happened, and so I broached the matter as we ate the smoked chicken he had brought along.

"I am sorry for what happened earlier today."

"What?" he said through a mouthful of meat.

I regarded him closely, but there was no hint of pretense in his eyes.

"You left here angrily this morning. Don't tell me you have forgotten."

"Oh, that?" he asked, and continued eating. "It is bygone. Forget it."

I considered foregoing the matter as he said or to press on in a bid to iron out any misgivings, no matter the trace, that might be lodged somewhere in the wide expanse of his heart.

"I want you to understand that I don't hold anything against you as an individual, and I can swear that a lot of diaspora Africans yearn for a time when they can be like the both of us, trusting in our kinship and in the knowledge and warmth of it. If our governments can make this happen, I am sure that the world will be a much happier place for the African wherever he may find himself, in either the Caribbean, Africa, South America, North America or Asia."

A mischievous smile was on Michael's face when he looked up from the food. "You know you sound like a politician already."

"No, I don't sound like any of those fuckers. What I am actually saying is no different from what Marcus Garvey, Bob Marley and other African leaders of thought had envisioned for the African race. A unity. One that is solid, and founded upon a knowledge of ourselves."

"I get you, bro. You are right. I have never thought about things in this way you are making me see it. But truth be told, you are right. For me, however, I don't want to be a politician. I don't want to bother myself with all of it. It is too messy for me. To be honest with you, I don't see myself relocating to Nigeria after my studies. It is best to love that country from afar. And my opinion goes for the rest of the continent. Joseph Conrad may have been right when he called it The Heart of Darkness."

"I am disappointed to hear this from you, bro."

"You don't have to be, my brother. Eat the chicken. Enjoy it while it is still warm. The problems of the world will still remain even by the time we are done eating it. So, don't stress yourself."

SIX

Kay koule twonpe solèy, men li pa twonpe lapli

Donate to Save Africa, a sign read. It was positioned on the sidewalk so that whoever walked up High Street would see it. Intrigued, I stopped to read the sign further. It went on to say that millions of Africans were dying of starvation and went on to direct passersby to drop in their donations through a slot in a box. I dipped my hand into my pocket.

"What are you doing?"

I turned to Michael. "I am sure I have some loose change."

"Look at you," Michael said, and laughed. "This is a scam."

"How you mean?"

"So you think that scamming schemes are restricted to only when it is about the narrative of some Nigerian prince? Please come. Let's continue to our destination. This one is a local European scam."

A part of me didn't want to believe Michael but his conviction was overpowering and so I fell in step beside him.

"So, tell me," I said. "How is this is scam? You mean to tell me that the donations will never get to Africa?"

"Do you know how many aid agencies are in Africa already?"

"But that does not answer the question."

"Well, all I am trying to say is that I can bet my money that those donations will likely end up in European bank accounts and not a dime of it will get to Africa."

"Now, this is serious."

"You have experiences enough to not be naive. Was it not you who enlightened me on the gangsterism that France pulled on Haiti for over a century whilst the world watched on? Do you think Haiti is the only country that has witnessed European gangsterism? If these people know what their own people do in other nations, with the blessings of European governments, they will realise that they lack the moral credibility to preach all they do about fairness and advancement in the world."

"Michael, I think you have a point."

"Why did you have to call my name?"

"What?" I asked, at a loss.

"Why did you have to say *Michael, I think you have a point*? Why not simply say it without mentioning my name?"

"And what is wrong in mentioning your name?"

"It made me feel as though I was talking to a professor, a doctor, a lawyer, something like that. I mean, someone whose displeasure could make life difficult for me."

I laughed. "You are crazy, you know."

"Yes, I know."

Nighttime met us at the pub in the company of Anabelle and her friends. It was a Tuesday night, and the pub was not as filled up as it usually is. To one far end of the club, a cluster of youngsters had their attention to the television where a football match showed. They were fans of one of the teams and now and then they would break into a chant in support of their team, thus drowning every other sounds in the pub. At our table, we would fall silent until the chant ceased since it was pointless holding a conversation in that time. Gladly, none of us had any interest in football.

"Let us go play pool," Josy suggested, indicating a snooker table to one corner of the pub. I had noticed the table earlier because a handful of heavily built hipsters had been noisy while they played. Now, there was nobody there and the place was empty.

"I don't know how to play," I said. If that was meant to discourage Josy, it didn't. Even Suzy indicated interest.

"It is a good thing you are not a pro. We will teach you. It will be more fun," she said.

"Come, let's take up the place before someone else does," Josy beckoned, and getting off her bar stool and taking up her drink, she led the way in that direction.

From the entrance of the pub one would think that the corner with the snooker table was much smaller than it actually was.

On getting there, I saw for myself that it was a fairly spacious corner lit by a coloured pink bulbs that gave the place a feel quite removed from the general ambience of the pub. There were three snooker tables properly spaced apart to make room for a cluster of players around each table. Padded lounge chairs were built against the way round about, evidently to allow for spectators. Here and there, tall bar stools took up spaces. I hung my coat on one of the coat hangers and took out stick which Josy handed to me even as Suzy went about setting up the balls.

A few minutes into the play and I was already enjoying it. Josy, better experienced, was patient with walking me through the process, but it didn't stop her from enjoying the good whipping that she was giving me. Suzy was also there to give me assistance and cheer me up, but I could also tell that she also enjoyed it that I was losing. But surely she was enjoying the game more than Josy because assisting me meant that we had our bodies close to each other and would steal kisses every now and then.

To another table, Anabelle was having a difficult time keeping up with Michael. A mischievous grin was perpetually plastered on his face as he reveled in Anabelle's frustration.

The night wore on like this until it was time to leave the pub. Outside, the atmosphere had turned chilly. Youngsters smoked as they walked about, in groups or pairs, some drinking and almost everyone smoking. A crackhead was talking at the top of her voice. There was no telling how long he had slept in his clothes. Hysterically, he walked up to us.

"Hey, mates. Can I have a cigarette, please? A cigarette. Any to spare?"

I began to explain that I didn't smoke, but Suzy led me on, to catch up with Michael and Annabel who were already paces ahead. Josy caught up from behind as she had lingered on to put on her coat.

"Let's go check out somewhere else?" she suggested.

"Where do you have in mind?" Anabelle turned to ask.

"Up the street … Forgotten the name, but it is just up the street. Let's go."

We walked a good twenty minutes, from my calculation, talking as we did and avoiding brushing against many other fun-seekers on the sidewalk. Oxford is always that way. The streets had a way of coming alive at night with young people obviously freed from whatever engagements held them hostage in the day. It was as though the adults had the streets in the day but would give up sidewalks at night for youngsters.

Josy took us to a club, but the bouncer wouldn't let us in.

"We are at full capacity now," he said grumpily to Josy.

"So, what do we do now, bro?" Michael asked.

The bouncer, ignoring Michael, directed his reply to Josy. "You will have to wait outside until someone else leaves the club. It is the rule."

I wouldn't have cared, but while Josy and her friends were pissed, Michael was incensed as he insisted that the bouncer was racist and wouldn't let us in because as Africans we were in the company of European ladies.

As though to buttress his point, two ladies in revealing silky dresses and high heels alighted from a taxi and walked up straight to the bouncer, who held open the door for them with a bow.

Apparently, it was either they were regulars, or he was expecting them. Loud music mingled the sound of merriment seeped out of the open door and was permanently cut off with the door being shut, as though to let us know that beyond the door was the world we yearned for, and which was completed separated from where we stood. The incidence, as we observed it, proved too much for Anabelle and her friends to stomach. They rained abuses and threats on the bouncer who went on looking straight ahead, indifferent to their presence. They could well have been screaming at a statue of Gandhi.

We were already creating a scene, and it rested on Michael and me to convince Annabel and her friends to come away. It was pointless allowing things get out of hand and getting the police involved. I just don't like the police or getting involved with them.

Policemen were the same to me, wherever the clime, and I am sure Michael feels the same way too. He had told me enough about how brutal the police in Nigeria are, and how one would always do well not to allow them to get involved in his affairs.

By the time we approached another establishment, Annabelle and her friends were sufficiently calm. It was Michael who had led us on. The place was an African pub and everything about it oozed Afrocentrism; from the decor and the paintings hanging on the patterned walls to the fabrics of the chairs and tablecloths. The burly bouncer at the door shook us warmly and we were charmed into the ambience almost immediately. At some elevated platform, a DJ treated the place to African hip hop. Most of the customers were Africans except for a sprinkling of Europeans who obviously had come in the company of their African friends. Michael was already in his element. He nodded to the beat of the music and Annabel felt impressed. I considered it quite touching to see how genuinely impressed she was about my friend's happiness, and now and then she attempted to dance along with him but failing to move in synchrony with the music, would give up the effort with an amusing laugh.

Flanked on both sides by Josy and Suzy, I compared myself with Michael seated across in the booth with Annabelle. While I seemed to have more, yet he was content and apparently happy with Annabelle.

For me, I had to divide my attention cautious not to push one away with favourtism for the other. It felt like a burden which I would have to bear with tact. For a moment I blamed Michael for my predicament. Earlier I had seen it as an added gain, but now I was beginning to see it for what it was - a predicament, just as one would have a terminal disease that they were told was incurable but manageable. And it struck me that I would have to assume this role, the role of a polygamist, to be able to maintain the balance; for the balance is the basis upon which Michael and his girl's relationship - if I could call it that - lies. In the event that I backed out of my role, then it would be as easy for Michael and Annabelle to hang out as they pleased. I was the bonus. And certainly where Michael had a chance of building something lasting with Annabelle, what chance did I have? Certainly neither Suzy nor Josy would develop genuine affection for me, women being the jealous gender that they are, and rightly so. I was an amusement, a distraction, useful for as long as the need lasted.

"What can I get you?" a waiter asked. She was Eastern European. There was no mistaking the sharp facial features.

I ordered for a beer, same as Michael. The girls ordered for their drinks. Soon our drinks arrived and as we drank, we talked, cuddling and kissing. Every other booth was taken and all around us, people appeared to be talking, kissing and having a good time except for one bearded and bespectacled fellow at a lone table who caught my eye.

He was such a person who commanded attention in a room of people. He had an afro that stood out tall in spikes reaching as far up as his full beard reached downwards. Definitely he was West African. The cheerfulness of his clothes gave that away about him. It has been said that only West Africans wear bright fabrics and I have never had reasons to refute it. His clothing was custom-made, looked expensive and were as elaborate as the beads on his arm and neck. Although it was hard to tell, but I wagered he was in late thirties or early fifties. A waiter came to him, placed a cocktail before him and momentarily interrupted him from his phone. He treated the waiter to a friendly smile and handed her his card to paid with. She was back moments later with his card and receipt.

Our eyes caught and I waved. Every other at our booth caught the gesture and this earned the man some more pair of eyes from my direction. He nodded at me in acknowledgement and continued on with his drink.

Excusing myself from my company and went over to him.

"Hello, how are you?" his boisterous voice thundered, taking me by surprise.

"I am fine."

"Oh, please do sit," he said, waving me to the seat opposite him.

"My name is Jean Claude," I began as I sat, extending my hand. He took it.

"That sounds very French. Where are you from? Surely not Senegal."

"No. I am from …"

"Comoros?"

"Haiti."

"Oh … Haiti."

"So, what brings you to Oxford? Studies?"

"Yes. I am studying anthropology at St. Anne's College."

"Impressive." Then recollecting himself. "Sorry, I didn't introduce myself. My name is Chukwuemeka. I am an academic visitor here."

"Are you Ghanaian?"

"Nigerian."

"Oh, nice. The second Nigerian I am meeting here."

"Oh yea?"

"My friend over there is Nigerian," I said, gesturing at Michael.

Over in his booth, Michael was busy keeping the girls' company. He was having a good time and so didn't notice nor acknowledge our attention turned momentarily his way.

"Your friends are students too?"

"Yes."

We talked a great deal so that I forgot all about Michael and the girls.

Chukwuemeka, as I learned, was an academic and was well travelled. He had also been to Haiti, and that was before the earthquake.

I think it was because he had visited Haiti that I got endeared to him.

It was the first time ever I was meeting a Nigerian who had visited my country and who was very knowledgeable about the place.

One thing though that I learned quickly about Chukwuemeka, was that he spoke his mind and cared nothing about how his listener felt about it.

I guessed it came with the territory - that for a person to be an academic of his status, the one would have gotten used to telling people about his unpleasant findings to the point that considering people's feelings would matter little to him. After all, he was no politician. As say in Haiti, a leaky roof tricks the sun, but it does not deceive the rain.

By the time, Chukwuemeka stood up to leave, he gave me his card and told me to come visit him any time. I clutched on to the card, shook hands with him and watched him leave with a swagger.

Before pocketing the card, I took a look at it.

It read:

Dr. Chukwuemeka Kalu
African Studies Centre,
University of Oxford.

SEVEN

Kouri pou lapli, tonbe nan lanmè

On the next morning, I was at the African Studies Centre to see Dr. Chukwuemeka.

Since seeing his card, I had decided never to address him without his appropriate title. Not only because he had earned it - after all it was no easy feat - but then he looked too important to be addressed without his title.

It was nearing lunch time when I met with him and so he asked that I join him for lunch.

We walked the short distance to a Japanese restaurant, to the continuous stare of passersby taken in by his appearance as much as his clothing. Twice, people asked to take a picture with, and he obliged. It would appear that his presence added to the touristy feel of Oxford. But then, these distractions made our trip to the restaurant appear longer than it should.

In the restaurant, people would not stop staring our way and I couldn't help noticing.

As for Dr. Chukwuemeka, he was unperturbed and carried on as such. It would appear that, very much unlike me, he was used to being the centre of attention wherever he went.

When our foods arrived, I dug into my plate of rice with shredded chicken and some other add-ons that appeared as strange as they tasted good. Dr. Chukwuemeka had ordered a whole platter of foods and handled his chopsticks with such dexterity.

"I lived for a while in Hong Kong and Singapore," he explained to me, when I pointed to his use of chopsticks.

Impressed, I asked, "What did you go there to do?"

He dabbed his mouth with a napkin. "For Hong Kong, I went to have a presentation at the University of Hong Kong. As for Singapore, I was just curious. I simply went there, ate in a restaurant, took a walk around and then headed out."

"Really?"

"You will have to pardon me. They often say that I am weird."

I couldn't help myself from staring at my host. Watching him eat was a wonder in itself. One would think that it would prove a difficult task eating with such a lush beard as he had, but the food in his platter was almost gone and not a speck of food was to be seen caught in his beard.

And the manner in which he handled his chopsticks, the dexterity left me in awe. Signaling for a waiter who, like me, was stealing glances from a corner, Dr. Chukwuemeka ordered more noodles. "Won't you have some more?" he asked.

I shook my head. After our meal, he ordered sake. "It is a Japanese drink," he said. "It is made from rice and no different from *kai-kai.*"

And when he talked about Japan, he talked about it passionately. That he had done some work on Haruki Murakami's works, while at the Kyoto University.

"What's *kai-kai*?" I asked, taking a suspicious sip from the miniature cup that looked like it was made from clay.

"*Kai-kai* is a local gin in Nigeria. It is distilled from palm wine. You know palm wine?"

I wracked my brain. "Yes. It is gotten from palm tree."

"It is the sap of the oil palm or raffia palm," he explained, downing his *sake* in one go. "What they do is, they tap the sap from the palm and then they distil it to get *kai-kai.*"

"I see."

"You know," he said, adjusting in his seat, a gesture that I had learned so soon to signify his readiness to deliver a lecture. "The Japanese and every other culture of the world have learned to globalise their foods. They package these things and make them exotic and appealing to you. You could go into any stores in Oxford to see what I am trying to say. But for Africans, somehow we feel that the world will consider us uncivilized folks if we eat our foods in the open. We even shy from mentioning their names. Instead we find desperate ways to anglicize them and if that doesn't work, we ban them from being mentioned outside of our native circles. Don't you agree that such is a different height of inferiority complex?"

"I agree."

"We really should have *kai-kai* packaged and put on the global stage. We should call Udara what it is, rather than call it 'African star apple' or 'cherry'. When the European comes to a place and sees something local to the environment, he asks *what do you call this?* And when you tell him, he often doesn't try to anglicize it. This is why we have a name as kwashiorkor, because the European came to Ghana, and encountering the ailment for the first time, asked to know what it is called. But if it left for Africans to present a knowledge of the ailment to the world, they would have so tried to anglicize it and come up with something like *African atrophism syndrome."*

"Maybe they would call it *general atrophocondria"*

Dr Chukwuemeka burst out laughing. He laughed so hard and well, like one who had no care in the world, and this earned him glances from every corner. But it wasn't the sort of glances that showed indignation. I sensed admiration in them that one could be so light at heart and express it so.

"Remind me never to rely on your opinion for things like this," he said when he had recovered from his bout of laughter.

Our meal done, he paid and gave the waiter a generous tip.

I stepped ahead of him just in time, held the door for him and watched him breeze majestically past.

I did not see Michael until the evening of the next day when he came around to my place. There was a certain aloofness about him which I couldn't place. But it wore off soon after he had downed a bottle of beer from the pack he brought with him.

"What are your plans for this evening?"

I told him that I had no plans and that I would rather stay indoors and do some reading. A test was coming in a couple of weeks, and I was already behind schedule on the amount of work I should have covered.

"Do you have anything in mind for this evening?"

He shrugged. "Errrmm … not yet."

"What about your girl?"

"Who?"

"Annabelle. You plan on hanging out with her this evening?"

"No. There is another girl." He sat up and came alive with a burst of excitement. "She's Greek. You need to see this chic. Man! And she just newly came to Oxford."

"So, what happens to Annabelle?" I asked.

"Nothing," he said. I looked at him searchingly, unable to arrive at a solid conclusion on what he meant. "Bro, Annabelle is still there. No hard feelings."

"Anyway, it is not my business to pry, but I was already thinking you both have something going."

"How do I answer this now?" he asked, tapping his jaw in thought. "Okay, thing is, it is not as serious as you want to make it seem. Annabelle is still there. We are good. And a man's got to taste waters as he sails through life."

His grin was infectious as he spoke, and I could tell that there was no way anyone could talk him out a philosophy he had adopted on life. "Why not have a can of beer?" he asked, shoving the pack on the table over to me.

I took one, popped it open even as I knew that I would take forever to finish it one sip at a time. Michael took out one can and took a long swig and, then suppressing a belch, he wiped his mouth with the back of his palm.

"Did you get the news about Nigeria taking loans from China?"

He gave it some thought before answering. "Yes. Every other country takes loans. So, what's the big deal?"

"China has been dishing out loans to African countries and when they can't pay back those loans, China takes control of some part of their national assets. We have seen a pattern with Ethiopia and some other African countries."

"Those countries are not able to pay money that they borrowed so they have to pay somehow. I am sure they had an agreement before taking the loans."

"But in the case of Nigeria, isn't Nigeria rich?"

"Yes. Stinking rich."

"So, why take loans from China? Shouldn't Nigeria be the place to go to when African countries need loans?"

"Well, it is the fault of bad leadership. Nigeria used to help African countries in the past with loans and freebies."

"So, what changed?"

"Leadership. I just said so."

"And what could possibly bring about a change that we all desired?"

"Bro," Michael hissed. "Don't you get tired of all these things? You are here in England, far removed from the shit that is happening in Africa and yet you bother yourself over these things. See, you are here. There are no mosquitoes. No power cuts. It is secure and pleasant here, with lots of chics. You can stay out as late as you choose, and nobody stresses you. Why then are you stressing yourself? Have you eaten today?"

"I am not hungry."

"Are you sure?"

"Why the emphasis on whether I am hungry?"

"Because it is hungry people that get to angry over the slightest thing. Come, let's go eat."

"I told you that I am not hungry."

"But I am. There is this place. This chic took me there. Expensive but nice. You will like it. Come."

Running in the rain, falling in the river.

NINE

Pitit se richès malere

Word had it that Michael had grown up poor.

Actually, it was he who told me so. He was the second of four children, and as one would normally expect of second children, he was heady and always got into trouble.

His father, a junior ranking Customs officer, at the time would return home to news of how Michael's demeanour, and they often bordered around truancy or fights with other boys in the communal compound.

Once, it was reported to his father upon his return from work that Michael had smashed the window of a neighbour's Volkswagen Golf. And knowing how jealously the neighbour treated his car, which he always parked in the centre of the yard, for everyone to take notice of, Michael's father had practically gone mad, first with anger, and then with fear.

That night, he had beaten Michael so badly that it took his mother to intervene.

Michael said that after that night, he began to wonder if the man was truly his father, as it appeared to him, that the man was bent on erasing his existence from this world in that moment.

It had taken four months in payment installments for the broken window to be replaced and his father had intended for Michael to stay home from school punishment.

"It is your school fees for two terms that I have used in paying for that window," the man had said.

Evidently, he was intent on keeping Michael from attending school, as punishment.

It was also possible too, that the man, was only looking for an excuse to keep himself away from paying Michael's fees.

However, one month passed, and Michael, began to settle down, to the realization, that he would not be going to school for a while.

At first, it had hurt him, seeing other kids, leave the compound in the morning, for school.

But, when he settled into the new arrangement, his

mother started to raise concerns; concerns, which her husband treated with nonchalance, until she had done something about it.

One morning, she had marched a confused Michael to school, paid his fees and deposited him amongst his classmates in the classroom.

When her husband came out to learn about the new development, he shrugged with indifference and continued with his supper of the previous night's lean soup.

He was a man who had accepted his lot in life and didn't complain over it.

Cut your coat according to your size, had always been his most used adage.

And he would say to himself, "Children are the wealth of the poor."

It was not until Michael was twenty, that his father's fortunes, changed when he began to have an affair, with a top-ranking deputy in the Customs Service.

She had appointed him, to her official staff, and given him access to much more that was above his pay grade and clearance level.

And that had changed everything about his finances.

Michael's mother never complained about the affair, and her husband did nothing to hide the source of the grace that had come upon the family and which she so generously enjoyed.

She owned a Mercedes, wore the latest fashion and was certain of trips to Dubai for shopping and holidaying.

Nothing else mattered, after all people did much worse to feed and provide for their families.

The sudden change in the family's fortunes, was a most welcome development for Michael. He loved the duplex they now lived in Abuja. For neighbours, they had people who mattered.

Rich people.

The kind who took their children to London whenever schools went on vacation. Suddenly, there were no more power cuts. The streets in their area of town were paved and lined with trees. So serene was the environment that children skated on it in the evenings.

And the area was safe too.

There was no danger of policemen picking young men off the streets, hauling them onto waiting vehicles, to slam fabricated charges on them. Nobody shouted. There were not to be heard any sounds of generators. It was not that people didn't have generators, but they were big and soundproof in that part of town, not the kind you found elsewhere coughing and belling out smoke and screaming as though in protest. There was never to be found any shortage of cars in their compound.

He was to learn soon enough that they were confiscated cars from importers. There was also a warehouse where other confiscated items were kept until they were auctioned off for Customs officers like his father to share. But for the cars, his father usually brought them home, so that Michael always pulled up in school in a different car each day.

A shock came for Michael when his father had announced to him that he would no longer continue with university in Nigeria but would soon be leaving for England to study.

At first, Michael had protested.

Nigeria was good for him, and it was the one place where he could be seen for the somebody that he was.

He had friends and enjoyed so many privileges and would never give them up for anywhere or any school, even if it were Oxford.

"You will give everything up here for Oxford! That is where you are going!" his father had thundered.

And because Michael had protested, his father had grounded him and cut him off every privilege until he had succumbed five days later.

Begrudgingly, he had come to Oxford.

TEN

Tanbou bat nan raje, men se lakay li vin danse

You know, we always say that, the drum is beaten in the grass, but it is at home that it comes to dance.

Everyone talks about the earthquake in Haiti - the earthquake of 2009.

It is what comes to mind, whenever they hear about people of my country, and it makes me think that myself and my countrymen don't exist in the minds of people; as though we are a people living on the farthest edge of the planet, unseen, unheard of, until the earthquake happened, and musicians came together to sing *We Are the World.*

Surely, that could be the one thing that announced us to the rest of the world. *We Are the World.*

It didn't matter that we knew the world all too well - much of it - even though the world moved on with no knowledge of us.

And yes, the earthquake! It did more than what people imagined and saw on their TV screens. It made me, at least in a certain way.

The earthquake happened and I came out of the rubble of our home, alone - an orphan.

It took helping hands to get the rest of my family out of the debris, but they had gone limp and lifeless already, caked in cement dust and dirt.

Wherever you turned to, cries and wails reached you, and so when my family had been brought out, laid out beside the debris that had once been our home, it occurred to me that it would be pointless adding my voice to the already saturated atmosphere of desolation.

Maybe I would have cried too, but I had done all of the crying before then, for somehow I had had the premonition that my family were not making it out of the debris when a whole day had passed without seeing them. I was too weak. And it was when a woman began to tend to the gash in my head that I realised that I was injured too. She could have been a nurse. Or a doctor.

But there was no way of telling as she wore no uniforms, and like everyone else, she bore that sad look that told of a desperate attempt to keep from panicking. And as she tended my wound, I wanted to ask her about her family, if she had none, whether they were safe, or if they were trapped just as mine.

"*Shhhh*, keep quiet," she had told me. "Everything will be fine."

And then, I began to wonder, how she had known what I had wanted to say, or when I had said them.

Maybe I was in a trance of sorts. Maybe the earthquake hadn't happened, and I was dreaming.

Perchance it was a dream that had taken too long to come to an end, and I hoped somehow that any moment I would be roused from it. This was what I was thinking until the cloth that the nurse dabbed against my head cut stung. It stung so badly, and I thought it was more from the liquid with which the cloth had been dampened than from the cloth itself, and I thought that it stung that hard in a bid to remind me that I was very much awake and that I was in no dreamland.

"Sorry," she said, noticing my wince.

But I had begun to cry. I didn't know how it had started, but I noticed the tears welling in my eyes, building up and obscuring my vision until they began to hurry down my cheeks.

My nose, too, was running. I would sniff and try to

wipe away my tears, but each time I tried, the nurse's hand tending to my wound always got in the way.

They had already begun to take my family away. The men went about it, with an air of solemnity, going about like zombies, that had materialized from the rubble elsewhere.

First, they draped clothes over each body, and then carrying them onto makeshift stretchers, they took them in the direction of a waiting lorry some distance away where the road, although obstructed here and there by rocks and stones and parts of what had once been the roofing of houses, was still pliable.

"Your family?" the nurse asked. "Have you seen them?"

I pointed to the men carrying the last of my family in their stretcher and from the look of it, I could tell it was my mother; she alone was the big one of the two of my parents. And it struck me that that was the last I would know of them in the coming days and for all time. At that, I began to cry uncontrollably. The nurse stepped away, leaving me and my grief alone for a while.

There were many others like me. Boys, girls, little children and older ones. Many had wounds and some had lost limbs. I was among those that had survived with only a cut here or there. We were kept in a shelter that had once been an abandoned Baptist Church building. Everyone said that it was the house of God and that was why it had remained standing when every other building had crumbled when the earthquake had happened. For days and nights we stayed in the shelter and on many of those times, I could hear the priest sing:

On Christ the solid rock I stand,
All other ground is sinking sand …

Father Jean Doussou, was a French priest, who was tall, and so slender that his cassock hung on his frame and billowed on any windy day like a sail upon a mast. Rumours had it, that he came from a family, who made their money from questionable means, and that his choice to become a priest was an act of rebellion.

Nobody knew how true that was, but one had to hang around the priest long enough to see that he was a man given to fits of anger now and then. Had he not been a priest, it was all too clear that he would have been an oligarch or anything close to it: because he loved power and courted it. Yet he was a devout man, considering what was known and heard of other priests on the island.

ELEVEN

Manman chen pa janm mòde pitit li jous nan zo

Michael never knew much about me, mostly because he never asked.

He was the kind of person that was content with only what stared him in the face. Hardly did he question things; the typical young man who prefers to live at the moment and allows such as the past and future to remain in their respective realms. I wasn't seeing much of him as I used to, and he began to take good notice of it. One evening after I had not seen him for three consecutive days, I looked up from my book while seated in a cafe to see him standing in front of me.

"How far?" he asked in his characteristic manner, smiling. He settled into the seat opposite me without prompting and then held out his hand.

"I dey," I replied as I had learned to, accepting his proffered hand and ending the handshake with a s nap of our fingers just as he had taught me.

"Long time."

I shrugged, closing the page of *The Beginning of Everything Colourful* and putting it aside.

"How is that your Prof friend?" he asked.

"Which of them?"

"You are asking as though you don't know who I am asking you about," he said. "The rastafari one."

"Oh. He is Nigerian. Don't you know?"

"No. I thought he's Jamaican or something."

"I thought same too until I got close to him. He is a nice man. You should meet him too."

"And discuss what, my brother? I am not ready to be talking about books and things that fill my head with too many ideas," he said. "Meanwhile, what are you having?"

I pointed to my cup of coffee.

Michael peered into it. "It is finished already. Let us order some more," he said, signaling for a waiter before I could say anything.

Soon as our orders arrived, and he dove into it. He had ordered some croissants too. I could deduce that he hadn't eaten a thing all day from the manner he ate. Not one word parted his lips until he had downed everything, and then he sat back, a look of satisfaction that I had not known to be there evident all about him.

"So what have you been up to lately?" he asked.

"Nothing much," I said. "Just the usual goings and comings of each day." I scratched my scalp. "I am sorry that I have not been available all these days."

Waving me playfully away, he replied, "That is nothing. Some days are like that."

"So how have you been? What's up?"

"Cool. Everything is cool. Your girls are worried about you. Always asking after you."

"You mean Suzy and Josy?"

"Of course, man," he replied jovially. "Who else? Or have you gotten yourself some hotter chic whom you are keeping away from me?"

"Naah, man. Nothing like that."

"I won't begrudge you if you have gotten yourself some fresh girl. But I will pick offense if you keep from making the introductions."

"Rest assured, man. There is nothing to begrudge me for or take offense for. I am straight, man."

"Nice."

"So, you said Suzy and Josy ask after me?"

"Yes, you just went cold on everyone. Man, that's worrisome."

“So why didn’t they reach me on my cell? They have my number.”

“You mean they didn’t reach out to you?”

“No, man. They didn’t.”

“Weird,” he said thoughtfully. “Anyway, let’s put that aside. You will have to come around one of these days, you know.”

“Yea, I will.”

“What about tonight?”

“I …”

“Come on, don’t give it any thought. There is nothing there to think about. We are meeting tonight at the pub. I will come around to your place to pick you up. Your presence will be a surprise for the girls. Don’t fail me.”

Like we say in Haiti, *a dog’s mother will never bite her little ones to the bones.*

TWELVE

Dwèt ou santi ou pa ka koupe l jete

Dr. Chukwuemeka was the one who took interest in my story.

I guess it was because, as an academic, curiosity came with the territory.

And anytime we met, we would talk until one of us had to excuse himself to attend to something, but only when it was really pressing.

Evidently, I interested the professor a great deal, for he soon gave me access to all of his free time.

In the evening, I would ride the bus to his flat in Cowley where I would sit across from him in his study as we drank from anything he chose, from the wine rack that looked like a barrel.

It was him I told what happened after our stay at the Methodist Church, when the earthquake struck my country.

Soon as I arrived at the Methodist Church, it was filled to capacity. It was, however, reserved for only children, as I was later to learn, that some other facility was meant for housing adults, especially the injured ones.

We ran out of drinking water in no time.

The adults who tended to us said that medicines had run out too.

Every morning, they would cook over wood fire in the front of the church.

It was always a giant cauldron that was used, and then every child would be served.

You could tell that the firewood were mostly pieces of furniture and joinery that had been salvaged from the rubble, four women and a man attended to us, and Father Dossou always helped out.

We could see the weariness on the countenance of the adults who catered to us. One of the women would most times retire to a corner and cry. I guess she had lost her family too. Perhaps, she hadn't and it was the sight of endemic hopelessness that broke her every now and then.

As the days went by, our rations became smaller and

smaller and there were talks that very soon there would be nothing left to eat.

But just as the hint of panic swept through our devastated hearts and minds, there was also a rumour that help would soon come from abroad. Haitians abroad, they said, were rallying around to send help to the homeland and foreign governments were also interested in doing something about our situation.

Help came. It actually came sooner than we had expected. The air around the place came alive with hopeful anticipation when one morning, news began to spread that aids had come from abroad. Helicopters had arrived our country bearing water, food, medicine and other essentials.

Everyone was in high spirits and for a moment we forgot about everything that had brought our lives down in one devastating quake.

It seemed like Christmas.

The world had brought gifts and all the rumour which had brought hopelessness were forgotten.

Our rations increased. We were given new clothes. They felt fresh to the skin and smelled in a way that was both strong and soothing. Some of them had things boldly written on it. A kid had a sweatshirt that had a Superman print in front. We envied him his luck. Had it not been that he was a big kid, I am sure one of us might have attempted to steal the shirt from him or bully him into parting with it. He so cherished the shirt and carried himself about as though he was Superman endowed with the character's capabilities by virtue of wearing the shirt. We began to call him Superman from that first day when he got the shirt. Apart from the clothing, every child received a new blanket too. They gave us mosquito nets and little mattresses which he lined up in four rows in the church building. There were soaps and bottled water amongst the relief items that we received.

Our moods soured as would be expected of people so generously given new things that we forgot our dire states.

That evening, we buried our dead.

Far away from the rubble and what had once been our residential areas, men had dug fresh graves in a straight-line fashion and laid next to each grave a body wrapped in cloth and ready to be lowered.

Father Dossou was present, but it was the Catholic priest who officiated. I have forgotten his name.

A boy mentioned it to me then, but I forgot it almost immediately.

But I could recall that he was European and said so much of things that I didn't hear. The funeral ceremony was a short one but one that appeared to stretch endlessly. Not many people wept.

I thought it was, because there had been too much weeping in the past days, such that no one had anything left in them to spill out. But there were sighs and the mood was as sombre as would be expected of the circumstance.

We forgot for the moment about the relief materials, and some of the aid workers were there in the crowd witnessing the funeral. Among them were people with cameras; they took shots here and there even as the service was going on.

An old man in the crowd muttered something about people not having the presence of mind to honour the dead, and then he suggested that anyone who took any more shot of the event should be marched away but no one paid him no mind. And seeing as frail as he was there was no point imagining his capacity to make good on his suggestion.

A TV crew was there too. Not exactly there, but a few meters away, with the anchor having her back to us. At first the whole setup had been confusing; I had never seen a TV crew before then. But then, it took a little while for me to understand who they were. *CNN.* I could see that written on the jacket of the crew members.

I wondered if there was a chance that I could be on TV. Maybe that would be possible if I stepped out of the crowd, I imagined. A bit, just a little bit, I said to myself. But then I didn't budge from the crowd.

I remained where I was standing with other boys and the crowd of mourners listening to the Catholic

Priests recitations and wondering which of the endless line of shrouded corpses was a member of my family.

After the corpses had been lowered into their graves and covered with earth, everyone returned to their normal lives as they had known it since the earthquake. We boys were ushered back into the Baptist Church and kept busy by a woman who had volunteered to keep us busy.

Father Dossou had appointed her teacher over us, in the belief that our unruly young minds would turn out another disaster if we were to be left idly to ourselves. And so the volunteer was meant to teach us just anything, anything that would keep our unruly minds as little boys occupied so that we wouldn't turn upon one another and begin the kind of things that happened with Golding's *Lord of the Flies.* That afternoon, she was teaching us from the Bible about Peter and his colleague who met a blind man at the entrance of the gate called Beautiful and healed him. I had heard that story a good many times and it made me wonder why I should sit and allow myself to be regaled with the same story another time. But I dared not leave the church building else I could get a whipping from the teacher who also had soon begun to wield a cane.

"I want to go piss, ma," I told her with a stern look that otherwise marred what would pass for a beautiful face.

"You can go, but you must return in five minutes."

"Yes, miss," I said, grateful to be out of the hall that was packed with many other boys most of whom were so bored that they would rather lay back on their mattresses and sleep.

In the days that followed, we saw more and more food aid coming in that the coming and going of helicopters, ships and lorries laden with supplies became a common sight, and it didn't hold as much thrill as it held for us in the early moments after the earthquake.

But there was something about life that kept us from settling in, and if ever we began to settle into any situations, it came upon us and jostled us awake. That was how it felt - like I was being jolted out of comfort - when news came that some of us orphans would be taken away to new places, to be raised in orphanages. The news dampened our spirits as we had become bonded in a way that could be explained by the times in the evenings when we played football in the churchyard. Some of the boys were happy. They said we would be taken abroad where we would meet with foreigners and where life would be better for us.

They said we would get to see all of those places which we see only on TV screens. It was these things that made me begin to see the bright side of being moved to an orphanage away from Haiti and the rubble that much of it had been reduced to. I hoped I would be taken to

Canada or the US. Some kids said we would be taken to Germany. There were talks of other places too.

But nobody *was* certain.

We would only speculate, and speculation we did until some of us began to discuss, with certainty, our future as orphans in orphanages. They talked with a level of confidence as though were assured of anything. One said he would be going to the United States and there he would finally meet his uncle who had been away when he was yet a baby. He also said he would one day become rich and buy a house and cars in the United States. They talked highly in this manner, only getting sombre when they imagined that we all might not be taken to the same orphanage or country, even.

One week later, the transfer happened.

For me, I was boarded on a plane with three other boys who I was not familiar with.

It was Father Dossou who, holding my head, admonished me and the rest of the boys to be of good behaviour in the orphanage in France where we were being taken to.

He said to me: "Even if your fingers stink, you cannot cut them to throw them."

THIRTEEN

Tete pa janm twò lou pou mèt li

With Josy and Suzy, there was no telling what one was to look forward to, but they were their usual jovial lot when I met them that night.

Josy rushing over to envelope me in a hug, soon as I walked through the door. Michael had come around to my place that night as agreed and together we went to the pub.

"Runaway lover," Suzy said to me, and without getting off her stool, gave me a hug that ended with a peck on my cheek. "Where have you been?"

"I am truly sorry ..." I began.

"No need to apologize," Michael cut in. "Dude has been too studious lately."

"Don't sound like that, man," Anabelle said, giving Michael a playful swathe on the shoulder. "Cut him some slack."

"He is quite right," I said. "Lately I have been practically buried in work."

"That's understandable," Suzy said. "That's better than ghosting us."

"No, I can't ghost you girls," I said. "So what have you girls been up to?"

"First, we should order for drinks and then we can talk," Anabelle suggested, and everyone agreed that it was a great idea.

While we drank, we talked.

Our girls had not been up to much in the while I was out of touch. Their schedule had been practically the same; in the day they studied and went to class, and at night they came to wind down at the pub. They also talked about their plans of going to spend a week in Turkey.

"You guys should come with us," Josy said. "It will be fun, something different from what we are used to."

"Yes," Anabelle agreed, snuggling up against Michael who had his hand across her shoulder. "I will love to see Istanbul. And I have heard a great deal about Haghia Sophia."

"Turkey has so much history. We should all go see it," Suzy chipped in.

Michael looked to me, and I treated him to a look, that I hoped offered nothing. We had not foreseen this, and I wasn't ready to have myself cornered into making assurances that I was sure not to keep. We agreed with the girls that we would give it a thought.

The next morning, I returned to my place, and some brown envelope on the floor caught my eye.

It must have been pushed through the mail slot in my door.

Stopping down to pick it up, I flipped it over to see that it had the markings of some mail company. But the name on it wasn't mine.

It was a woman's. Surely the occupant of 3B, the flat further down that was sometimes mistaken for mine which was a number 3.

I hefted the enveloped, weighing. It was light. Maybe it contained some letters. Could be something that had to do with bills? But it didn't have the sender address of the Council Tax people or the electricity company. Tossing the envelope back on the floor, I continued into my apartment. I was spent and in dire need of a shower, some breakfast and some sleep as I had been up all night, drinking and discussing and expending what else was left of the night in having a good time with Suzy and

Josy while Michael and Anabelle had the balcony, and then Anabelle's room, to themselves.

I had taken a shower and heated up some pizza in the microwave when a knock got me hurrying to the door. It was a delivery man. Pakistani, I guess, but with a look that was in sharp contrast to the rare fine weather of that morning. He looked the kind who was bored with life and who hated his job so badly. His grey coat gave off that look that made one think that he had slept in it for nights on end.

"Is this number 3?" he asked.

"Yes. Good morning."

"This is for you," he said, handing me a sizeable package and began to leave. I stood, at a loss for how the package had come about. Could it be that someone was sending me a surprise package? But then, who could that be? It wasn't my birthday; I wasn't celebrating anything, and even if I was, it would be the first time that anyone would be sending me such generous gifts. I flipped the package and saw that it had the markings of some independent wine and cheese store. The name on the package was some woman's, surely not mine. I had not ordered anything, and nothing as elaborate as this.

Quickly, I dashed out of the house in my shorts, regretting it almost immediately as the English cold lapped against my bare legs and arms. It was always cold in England at this time of the year even when the weather appeared sunny. I spotted the delivery man just as he got into a beat down Hyundai and slammed the door shut. He had just started the engine when I drew up to him and rapped on his window. Opening his door a fraction, he asked, "Can I help you?"

"Yes, please. I am afraid the parcel you delivered doesn't belong to me. It belongs to someone else at some other address."

"But you confirmed that it is your address."

"I am sure that there is a mistake somewhere. I never ordered for these, and I am certain there is a mix up."

"I have done my job and have delivered the package as I was directed by the company."

"So, what am I to do with this considering that it is not mine?"

He shrugged. "I don't know. But you can call the company and sort it out with them. I have done my job." He made to shut the door, but I had placed the parcel on the ground and held onto the door, stopping him. Had the door been wide open, I would have dumped the parcel in his car. But there was no way to do so as it was. "Gentleman," he said to me, "can I close my door?"

I knew that tone. It was the sound of a man who, although weak, was capable of causing some deal of trouble. He could call the police and attempt to level some charge against me. These immigrants in England, there was no way of trusting them when it came to dumping their deep-seated frustrations on some fellow immigrant.

Deflated, I stepped aside as the man shut his door and muttered something to himself, started his car and drove away. I was angry at him and wished to make him pay for the inconvenience he was causing me. How was I to bear the brunt of his frustration at his job? Was I the one who uprooted him from his home in Pakistan or India, to bring him to England to suffer the weather and deprivation? Fuming and marinating in these thoughts, I carried the parcel back into my apartment.

Back in my apartment I decided to put the incident aside for the moment.

My pizza had gone cold, and I would have to heat it up again. The thought infuriated me as I blamed it on the delivery man who appeared to have been sent to ruin my day. Realizing that I might not have an appetite for the pizza or anything for that matter anymore, I returned the pizza to the fridge and went to pick up the parcel where I had left it on the table.

I compared the name addressed on the parcel with the one on the envelope which I had stumbled upon earlier that morning. It didn't surprise me that they were the same. I felt relief at the discovery, even, for it meant that I would be killing two birds with one stone - if ever I spotted the bird, that is.

I dressed in protective clothing, and then bearing

the parcel and with the envelope in the pocket of my jacket, I ventured outside in search of the rightful owner of them. My search took me down lane next to my street that opened up into a park. Number 3B was the last house in the line of town houses. A woman on the phone answered the door at the first ring and when she saw me standing at the door, she got off the phone, a look of surprise evident on her countenance. I could tell that she was in her fifties, modestly dressed in skirts and a cardigan and spotting a necklace that looked to me as pearls.

"Good morning," she said, beginning to regard me with a hint of suspicion.

"This wrongly arrived at my address, and I am wondering if it should have been delivered to you instead."

"What is the name on the parcel?"

I called it out to her. "Oh yes," she said, relieved. "They are surely mine. And I was calling the store, but they kept insisting that I had taken delivery of my orders."

I kept the parcel at her doorstep, happy to do so and relieve myself of the inconvenience, and remembering the envelope, I fished it out of my pocket. "And this also belongs to you too."

"Oh dear," she said, stretching her hand to receive it. She had already begun to tear it open as I walked away.

Relieved that I had done away with the parcel and

the inconvenience that it meant for me, I returned to my pizza, and while it heated up in the microwave, my mind drifted to the events of the previous night and the girls' suggestion that we vacation with them for a week in Turkey. It was possible that Michael had taken the invitation seriously, but I would not be going along with them. I didn't have the means to, even if I wanted.

Unlike Michael, I didn't have that parents who sustained my life in Oxford, so as to make it breezy.

It would have been different if life had turned out in a way that it hadn't, what with the earthquake in my country and all that it had brought with it for me.

The ding of the microwave interrupted my thoughts.

I got out the pizza, poured myself a glass of milk and settled in to eat while keeping an eye on and my ears to the Al-Jazeera news commentary on my TV.

But soon, my attention wandered from the TV and my room.

It drifted onto a great many other things far away from my present environment. I couldn't say exactly when this had become a thing for me, but I had come to realize at a young age that my thoughts had a way of drifting from my environment. Michael had even told me that sometimes while we talked, I was transported elsewhere, especially when I got quiet.

Maybe he was right, and I was always never present at any given point for too long. It was either I dwelt in the past or in the future, and sometimes shuttling between the two within microseconds.

As you know, *breasts are never too heavy for those who have them.*

Quite mechanically, I ate as I ruminated in my thought, staring at the TV screen but never registering a thing. And when I had wiped out the last of the pizza and drained the last from the milk glass, I put away my cup, tossed the pizza pack in the rubbish bin and headed for the bathroom to take a shower. As the water beat down my body, I thought of Haiti and the first time I had come to France on that Red Cross flight.

FOURTEEN

Konn li pa di lespri pou sa

In France, it was different - *nothing like my teenage mind had conceived.*

We were brought to Mittelbergheim, which was a long distance away from Paris and anything I had dreamed of France.

And as we say in Haiti, knowing how to read, does not mean you have wisdom.

Before then, I had always thought of France with a sort of longing.

Excitement had claimed the better of me when myself and a host of other boys had been notified that we were being taken to France.

But we had landed at an airport and from there a bus had taken us on a long ride through rural France with endless views of vine fields with their stone houses, until at last in the evening we had arrived at the stone structure that looked like a chateau from the medieval era.

Drained and tired from the journey, I felt like crying at the sight. I missed home immediately and wished to be back in Haiti, among the rubble and everything I had been torn away from despite their hopelessness.

The orphanage, I was soon to learn, had once served as a monastery in time past and was now run by the Catholic Mission.

There were about thirty boys in the orphanage and apart from myself and ten others who had been brought with me from Haiti, there was only one other boy who looked like us, although the hue of his skin was of a different kind and his hair, woolly, stood out elaborate on his head.

We saw him shoveling fallen leaves into a wheelbarrow with three other European boys in shorts and shirt. But he was a reclusive one - this much could be noticed about him in an instant. The orphanage was run by a staff of about ten men and older women who saw to it that everyone was fed and did what was expected of them.

We were conducted about the place, given some new clothes and familiarized with the place. It was a bulky old woman with an accent that gave away her struggle to communicate the things she had to say that took us on a tour of the orphanage. She showed us about and familiarized us with what was expected of us at each moment of the day.

"In time, you will get used to the daily timetable," she said.

We were given new blankets and some new clothes. Just when she was showing us the chapel where we were to gather to say our prayers thrice every day, a bell rang. "Time for dinner," she said, and ushered us into a hall lined with three long wooden table with chairs on either side. There were boys of different ages seated on the tables. They were of different ages, some older than me, and others younger. But there was something about them that didn't sit well. Rather than being chatty and restless as expected of a cluster of that many boys their age, they were quiet and collected as though a certain melancholia held silent reign over every one of them.

"Find somewhere to sit down," she said with a gesture of her hand, and at that we knew that we were at liberty to choose any spot in the great hall to sit. Timid and skeptical like the newcomers that we were, all ten of us Haitians clustered about a table and sat like the rest of the boys. In that moment, a group of bigger boys laboured into the hall bearing steaming basins that held food. To a table to one side of the hall they settled their burden. Some other younger boys wheeled in carts bearing plates and cutlery. Then we watched as everyone seated filed before the boys at the end of the hall to each get a plate of food, and then they would return to their place at the table to eat in silence. Two guardians, both looking stern and soulless stood aloof, their countenance betraying no emotion. We watched the order with which the boys handled themselves and when it went to our turn, we each filed in front of the bowls of food and had our plates half-filled with oatmeal.

At night, we were shown where to sleep. It was a large hall that with narrow spring beds lined in two rows against the walls. The windows were kept open to let in the cool sweet air of fresh vegetation.

A bell rang out and all lights went out. I lay still in my bed, thinking and afraid to disturb the stillness that reigned about the place despite the number of boys present in that hall. Everything felt strange and I didn't like it. This was not what I had thought it to be. Not the earthquake. Not life. And surely not France. I felt torn away from everything I had known and expected. The other boys who had come with me from Haiti were apportioned bed in separate parts of the hall. We had been far flung, scattered, and I suspected this to be intentional; for what purpose, I could not tell. In the stillness of the night and with my thoughts for company I cried into my pillow, wishing that things could be changed and that I could turn back time to when all was as it was in Haiti, with my father and mother, before the earthquake. I wished the earthquake had never happened, that it could have been averted. Oh, I cried and cried until the lights came back on and the boys began to get out of their beds to give us a welcome that I had never expected.

FIFTEEN

Rayi chen an, men di dan I blan

Oxford is very much like very few cities in the world in that you exist in the present but amongst relics of the past, and when you moved about the city you are certain to get to certain points, where you become unsure whether you are an ancestor revisiting the paths he had tread.

I felt this way, when I made my way around the campus ground one morning.

My destination was the Weston Library, where Dr Chukwuemeka was to have a lecture on the caste system of Igbo land.

A glance at my watch told me, that I was right on time.

Blackwell's was already within sight and so it meant that a few paces more and I would be at my destination.

This is on Broad Street.

In one of our talks in his house, Dr Chukwuemeka, had told me about the Igbo caste system.

We were seated in the garden, in front of his house sipping the palm wine and eating the roasted groundnuts, he had ordered from an African vendor in London.

Dr Chukwuemeka maintained that evening, that every society functioned in such a way that guaranteed that everyone does not belong to the same class, despite every talk on egalitarianism.

To him, the concept was elusive, a utopia and one that is held out to the masses intentionally because it served a select few when the masses had their heads in the clouds.

According to him, the Igbo people, ignorant of the systems theorized by Europeans, were already doing almost the same things that the Brits presently have; a class system.

He said in Igbo land, the Ozo caste is different from the Diala and Dibia who in turn are different from the Osu, Ume, and Ohu. But it is not exactly like what you have in India, he had maintained.

Hurrying up the elaborate steps, dotted by people seated about in the sun, I found my way into Weston Library.

It was right across Sheldonian Theatre. Before the Oxford Martin School.

The Bodleian Library, is one of those inventions that seemed to envelope you in its embrace, once you walked into it, and depending on the situation, it could strike you as snobbish, not so much for the architecture than for the cultural importance which it effortlessly exudes.

Walking past the cafe, shelf of books and historical relics displayed in glass cases on the walls I continued in the direction of the hall.

The lecture had already begun as I settled into a seat I was lucky to find at the furthest end of the small hall.

It appeared that more people than me were interested in learning about the Igbo caste system but more surprising was the realisation that there were only four Africans to be spotted about the hall.

The others were most likely Brits. And unlike Africa, they were as conscious of their own history as they were of learning about others.

Little wonder that there was more knowledge on Africa to be found in the Britain, than there were to be found in Africa. And someone had mentioned that if anyone needed materials on African history for research or documentary purposes, they were to be found in the libraries and archives in Britain and never in Africa.

I got my pen and began to jot points from the lecture.

Dr Chukwuemeka was elaborate in his descriptions and many times he made the audience laugh.

I had come for the lecture mostly out of curiosity.

If they said that the most of native Haitians were Igbo people, then it was only right that I understood and familiarized myself with the political and social history of my ancestors.

A lady in the audience asked a question. She was Igbo and she made it a point of note to introduce herself as being a doctorate fellow at Harvard and had only been privileged to be visiting at the moment.

She wanted to know if it made any sense to dismantle the class system and strive for an egalitarian society which every democracy was seeking to model itself after.

Dr. Chukwuemeka's replies didn't sit well with her, but it appeared she was willing to let the matter slide for the time being.

At the end of the lecture, I waited at the back of the hall, as people from the audience went to greet Dr Chukwuemeka and shake his hand, telling him how enlightening his lecture was.

Some of them had some questions to ask which they had not for whatever reason asked during the question and answer session. There were some who came to take pictures, and Dr. Chukwuemeka obliged them, smiling at the appropriate time at the cameras. All the pleasantries dragged on until it appeared to me that I would have to wait for all eternity to be able to reach the professor.

At last, everyone left the hall, and I went over to Dr. Chukwuemeka just as he was packing his things into his leather bag.

"Oh, you came?" he asked, looking up at me.

"Yes, Prof," I said, helping him pack up his things.

"I am surprised that you took the liberty to come. This topic is no new thing to you. There is nothing I have told the audience that I have not told you already, and I bet that you know much more than I was at liberty to say in the course of this lecture."

"I know, I just wanted to come."

"Not that I don't appreciate your coming to occupy a seat at this lecture, but could it be that you have nothing else slated for this moment?"

"I am free at the moment. I have no classes and no other engagements."

"Great. In that case you won't mind keeping me company over coffee."

It was to the cafe in the Weston Library that we went to.

At the counter, the service lady took a liking to Dr. Chukwuemeka. She smiled at him generously and engaged him in small talk.

She was a Polish, she told him, and when she told him her name, she had laughed as he sampled it repeatedly on his tongue.

When asked how long she had been in the UK, she said ten years. She had come alone to study and had left her divorcee mother back in Poland.

In those ten years, she had not visited Poland, but she hoped to visit soon.

"I will have coffee and then this and this," Dr Chukwuemeka said, pointing at the pastry on display.

And then turning to me, he asked, "What will you have?"

"The same," I said, to which he treated me to a quizzical look that made me laugh. Saying our momentary goodbyes we took our orders to a table that offered us a view of the streets and settled down.

"Do you like it here?" Dr Chukwuemeka asked after sampling his coffee and setting it down.

"You mean this place?"

"Yes, all of it. Oxford."

I nodded. "I think so."

"Are you certain that you like it here?"

"Yes. I like this place."

"What do you like it for?"

I wracked my brain in search of an answer that would not lack in depth. "The place is great … The people are people that matter … I think the place has some prestige to it that opens doors everywhere."

"Now, that last part, my friend, is the thing. Look around you," he said, gesturing with a wave of his hand. "Everywhere about this place, you find people of all races who are drawn by the common goal of exerting some influence wherever it is they had come from. And do you know why that is?"

"No."

"Social class, my friend. People have learned from the inception of communal living to distinguish themselves from the masses. They create status symbols and limit access to it. This is an explanation in its crude form. With modernity, there is a lot of deception. Things are hidden in plain sight. Men have devised this. And this is why Oxford is what it is, and not everybody can gain access to this place or of being an Oxonian."

"I understand," I said, knowing full well that the Professor was in his natural element already.

"And do you think Oxford is any different from any other universities in the world?"

"According to the world ranking, yes. This place has maintained top position on the global ranking of universities. But I will not exactly point to how different it is from any others."

"It is culture, my friend. The Brits are a wise people. They built a culture around this university. The greatest of theirs have passed through these walls. And they have ensured over time that there is a strong history to this place. I envy them. Imagine if Kemet, Sudan or Timbuktu in Mali had retained their cultural history as centres for learning, and then we can say, *here in this walls of this citadel of learning, Aristotle and the best of Greek philosophers drank of their first taste of knowledge!* Imagine what that would mean."

I nodded. "It would be phenomenal."

"But we don't have any of such things."

"They were destroyed by invading Europeans and Arabs."

"True, most of them were destroyed by invading colonialist forces. But we can go on casting blames and not take responsibility for the edifices we destroy with our own hands because it is either we are after modernity in the belief that the old has no place in the new, or we destroy them because they are not in line with our borrowed spiritual views. Do you know how many cultural and spiritual edifices have been destroyed in modern times in Africa by priests and clerics of African descent?"

"It is the same in my country. People have always been against Voodoo. They say it is witchcraft. The church hates it just as the colonialist French hated and attacked it."

"But what do you think of it?"

"Of what?"

"Voodoo?"

"Urmm …" I shrugged for want of what to say.

"You are indifferent to it, I see."

"Yea, sort of."

"That is understandable," he said, biting into his pastry and chewing away.

"Do you know about Voodoo?"

"Not so much as to be an authority in it, but I practise voodoo. Europeans may not like it, but just as they have the right to practise their own spirituality, everyone else does have the same right. Voodoo for me is a most practical form of spirituality and has nothing to do with dogma and the trappings of it. Don't make the mistake of thinking however that I am marketing voodoo to you, my friend," and then he gave me a mischievous wink just as he raised his coffee to his lips. "So, tell me about the friends you keep here. What kind of people are they?"

"I don't have many friends."

"Ahh! Just like me. Really unfortunate."

"But there is a Nigerian friend I have. Michael is his name."

"He is a good chap, I guess."

"He is manageable."

Dr Chukwuemeka laughed. "That will do."

"I am still curious about how you came by a knowledge of voodoo."

"You think it is practised only in Haiti?"

"I have never thought about it so."

"It is practised very well in Benin Republic. They have this voodoo temple there that is quite a touristy spot. Voodoo is practised everywhere you find indigenous Africans, whether in Nigeria, Benin, Jamaica, Ghana, Gabon, you name it. I have been to Haiti, Jamaica, Cuba,

Brazil, not to mention all over Africa, and that is why I can say this."

"I remember you have been to Haiti."

"Oh, yes."

"It is not common to see a continental African who had been to Haiti."

"Yes, I went there in 2019, that was two years ago, before the pandemic grounded me in South Africa."

"What do you think of my country?"

"I was disappointed," he said. "I had gone there thinking to see something different, but it is exactly the same thing with Nigeria. The people, the place, everything … the same. I even heard Nigerian music playing from speakers. Everything felt like I was in Lagos. And it was there that I learned some more about voodoo."

"Did you meet with the practitioners or what?"

"Yes. I met with people who practised voodoo. Priests and priestesses. We talked and shared knowledge. Theirs is deeper, I must confess, and it is mostly because you folks have held onto it through successive generations. I also got some materials and books on voodoo which have helped me immensely.

Surprisingly, I found a similar book on the topic in Weston Library."

"You mean there are books on voodoo right here, in this place?"

"You can go see for yourself. You have an access card, right?"

"No, I don't."

Dr. Chukwuemeka searched in the folds of his robe and got out an access card. He handed it over to me. "You can borrow it for the moment. I will be headed home now to sleep off the rest of the day. Bring it back in the evening because I will be needing it tomorrow."

"Thank you," I said. And said to myself, "We can hate the dog, but we can not say that he smokes."

SIXTEEN

Bwa pi wo di li wè lwen, men grenn pwomennen di li wè pi lwen pase l

When we had finished our early lunch, Dr Chukwuemeka bid farewell to the Polish waiter, I saw him off to a waiting Royal Car. It was a blue Toyota.

Reiterating my promise to return his access card later that evening to his house, I bade him farewell as the taxi pulled into the slow traffic towards Broad Street, and then I turned around, bounded up the steps into Weston Library building, elated at the prospect of finding out what the shelves of Weston Library had for me with regards to the issue of voodoo.

The revelation, of the possibility, that there were to be found books on voodoo, in a guarded citadel of knowledge, as the Weston Library, appeared intriguing to me, more so because the French and Eurocentric spiritually had gone so far as to wage physical war on voodoo in my country.

But then, I reminded myself of what Dr Chukwuemeka had once said about everything to be known about Africa being hidden away in British museums and archives.

They understudy Africans, even the part of us that they frown about, they make it their business to know.

I am sure they do the same not for only Africans, but for the rest of the world and any such people who are subjects of interest.

At the entrance of the library, I swiped the access card and was granted entrance. The sheer amount of books about the place struck me with awe. If books are magical, walking into a hall filled with the rarest kind of books was a universe in itself.

And so, I stood, soaking in the view and losing myself in the thought that I had stumbled into a world of indescribable wonder and magic and that there would be no desire to return from it.

Just when I had decided to find some attendant, who would point me in the direction of what I had come to look for, a man began to make towards me.

From his composure, I could tell that he was a security man.

"Can I have your access card, please," he said to me, and my speculation was confirmed.

He was indeed a security man and already I wasn't liking the sternness behind his air of civility.

"Is there a problem, sir?"

"I would like to see your access card," he maintained.

I obliged, handing my access card to him while sensing trouble.

For a moment, I considered bolting for the exit, but things were past that stage already.

There was no going out for me yet.

Perchance this was nothing and I was already working myself over for no reason.

The man looked at my card and pocketed it.

"Is there a problem?"

"Whose access card is this?"

"Mine … sorry, my friend's … I borrowed it for the afternoon."

"I would like for you to come this way with me."

"You haven't told me if there is a problem with the card. I can call my friend to have it resolved."

"Sir!" the man said in a collected and firm manner, gesturing that I followed him. I did, even as I began to attempt to talk him into reasoning with me.

We had barely gotten to the security stand before I noticed a pool car pull up at the entrance of the library.

Two policemen got out of it, bounded up the steps and came towards us. The security man talked to them briefly.

"You will have to come with us, sir," one of the policemen said.

"Where?"

"To the station."

"Can I at least make a call?"

"Don't worry sir. It is nothing. Everything will be resolved at the station."

It was the Oxford University Security Services.

I was taken to the Thames Valley Police Station.

And made to wait at a reception.

From the look of things, mine would not be too much of a serious offence because I saw others have it worse.

Next to me, a man was seated, cuffed.

But he was already asleep, unbothered, weathering the stormy situation and whatever it held out for him.

He was probably drunk.

Across from me, was another young man barely a teenager; cuffed too but fuming. He looked like one who was unrepentant and would cause damage to whomever was responsible for his arrest.

There was an old man in a tweed coat somewhere down the line, and from the look of him, he was intent on ignoring everyone and everything around him.

I went over to a water dispenser, poured myself a cup and returned to my seat to drink.

It was then that I saw the news on the TV that President Moiise of Haiti, had been assassinated.

Something must have given my shock away, but I came to notice that my cup was on the floor and the water that it held was spilled all over.

Everyone at the police station had their attention on me.

Even the cuffed man who had been asleep was wide awake and I could see the extent of his attention on the television screen.

The newscaster said that President Jovenel Moise had been brutally assassinated in his home.

There was a footage of his wife, The First Lady, being wheeled into an ambulance.

According to the newscaster, investigations were underway to determine who was behind the brutal assassinations.

The news got everyone talking. They had come to realize the extent of my shock. One of the policemen said that it was unbelievable, even despicable, for a serving president to be assassinated in his home as it would take a lot of guts to do so. The sleeping man in the cuff began to ask me questions. Clearly, he had never heard of Haiti.

“Is it in Africa?” he asked. And so I began to tell

him about Haiti. As I told him, everyone at the station suspended their businesses to listen. I think they felt for me that I had lost a president and the only way they could show their respect at the moment was to listen.

I told them about how my ancestors had lived on the island as slaves brought in from West Africa, the revolution that had given us our independence, the debt that the French made us pay for our freedom, the never ending sanctions by the West, and the earthquake.

But then they were more interesting about me; how I had come to be in Oxford, and so I began to tell them about how life had changed for me with the earthquake and how I had come to France as an orphan and everything that happened in that time.

As we say in Haiti, the tallest tree says that it sees far, but the seed that travels says that it sees even further.

SEVENTEEN

Pa mòde dwèt ki ba w manje

Everyone knows this saying in Haiti: Never cut off the finger of the one who gives you food.

Even William Golding was very much right in insinuating with his book, *Lord of the Flies* that given an absence of a higher law and order, any group of people could retrogress into a primitive state from where they work their way towards the establishment of a new order.

And that was exactly how it was in the orphanage.

In the presence of the guardians, there was the established authority and order that caught the attention of any newcomer just as it caught mine on that evening I arrived at the orphanage.

But the moment it was lights out and the guardians were out of the way, I saw a different orphanage that wasn't the kind that I had thought it to be. In the absence of the guardians, there were boys amongst us who called the shots, and they wasted no time to drive home this point.

Hands held all of us newcomers, positioning our backsides prone on the bed. Before we could realize what was going on, our mouths were stuffed with used stockings that made us worry which was worse: the taste or the stink of it. But the socks in my mouth became the least of my concern when my shorts were pulled down to my knees and my bare behind was whipped repeatedly with what I was later to know as socks stuffed with pebbles.

The boys giggled as I writhed and at my muffled cries. They told me that it would be worse for me if I called the attention of the guardians to what was being done to me and my brothers that night. I could consider myself dead if that ever happened, they told me.

"Bear it in quiet like a man," one of the boys, heavily freckled with hair that reminded one of a locust infested cornfield, said in crisp French.

The next morning, I could barely walk properly.

It was the same with the ten of us who had come from Haiti. Every other conducted themselves in a manner that suggested that they knew nothing about the previous night and as to the reason why all Haitian newcomers appeared suddenly to waddle rather than walk.

For a moment, I thought that they really knew nothing about what happened that night, and that it might have been a bad dream which I had arrogated so much importance to, but the pain in my behind reminded me constantly that the previous night was as real as my fear that I might have finally arrived in hell.

And as for our guardians, if they noticed anything about the Haitian newcomers, they never showed it. That was when it began to sink in that clearly that was an established authority about the place, and I would do well not to challenge it. And so from that morning, I went about my business in quiet. My fellow Haitians also kept to themselves individually. They wouldn't look anyone in the face. And they seemed unwilling to talk but simply went about doing what they were told, grateful to be left alone and allowed to live at least.

The boy with the nappy hair that stood out on his head - the one I had caught sight of the first day we arrived - his name was Napoleon. It was he who told me his name. He had borne witness to the night of our initiation. That was what he called it. Initiation. They had done the same to him too, he told me. It was nothing personal. I was by myself when Napoleon approached me days later and offered me an apple. He had been assigned to the orchard and had stolen an apple during break time. He told me to eat it in hiding and that if ever I was caught, I should never mention that he gave it to me.

"What if they knew that you gave it to me?" I asked.

"They won't know. I will deny it that I ever gave you an apple from the orchard."

"And what will they do?"

"They will call you a thief. Your life will be difficult in this place. You will clean the toilet every day until another person commits an offense, then you will be free to live normally again."

"And what if another person doesn't commit an offense?"

"You will keep on cleaning the toilets and doing all the work that no one else will want to do."

I was soon to know that Napoleon was too curious for a quiet person. He asked a lot of questions. Sometimes he repeated the same questions after a while. It was a way to be sure that one was not being lied to, he told me.

He had learned it from Madame Beaumont the head of the guardians who was hardly seen except on occasions of great importance such as when one boy was to be adopted by a family or expelled.

It was said that she was always only seen when someone was about to leave the orphanage. Napoleon told me that countless times he had been on the brink of being adopted by some family, and twice he had nearly been expelled and that was why he had become one of the few boys to have seen Madame Beaumont a good many times. He told me that unlike me, he had never known any family. He had grown up in the orphanage.

The guardians had christened him, although he didn't know which of them had done the honour, or dishonour, but his guess was Madame Beaumont - for she was the most likely of them all to be so lost in her ideas as to think that some bastard mixed race child would amount to something as notable as the exploit of Napoleon Bonaparte.

No one had told him anything about his father or his mother and the closest knowledge he had of them was when one of the guardians in a fit of anger had called him the son of a whore, and went on to blame his mother for burdening them with the outcome of her whoring rather than take responsibility for it. He also said that one other certainty he had of his parents was that either his father or his mother was African. When asked which of his parents he suspected of being African, he said that it must have to be his father, because only a woman like the guardians would be too ashamed to associate with him, a mix-raced child.

I became friends with Napoleon and began to add *Bonaparte* to his name. And this, as I expected, made him laugh. It was one of those rare moments when he laughed. A serious and observant chap he was. He knew almost everything that went on in the place so much that he could predict everything that happened. It was he who told me that one of the guardians always crept into the outpost with the security man on night duty.

"Do you know what they do in there?" he asked, smiling mischievously.

"Of course, I know."

"Have you done it?"

"I won't tell you."

"Okay. Keep it to yourself, then."

One day Napoleon was called to see Madame Beaumont.

I was worried that he may have committed something grave especially as it was taking too long for him to return from Madame Beaumont's office.

And when eventually he did return, it was already late afternoon. He told me that a family had come to adopt him, and then noticing the sullen look that had come over me, he told me not to think much of it, as nothing would come out of it. It was the umpteenth time he had come close to being adopted but it had not come through and this would be no different. I wanted to believe him. I think I did. He told me that it was likely that he would grow into his twenties in the orphanage, and that at that age, Madame Beaumont would have no use for him again and would kick him out. That is what she does, he told me. But in the meantime, he was condemned to spending his entire childhood in the orphanage and not knowing what parenting or family looks like.

"What kind of family would you want to be adopted into?" I asked him.

"I have thought about this a lot. Sometimes I want this kind of family and the next time I want this other kind of family. But I think you have experienced what it is to have a family. Please, how does it feel like?"

I began to describe to him what it felt like. And because I had never given it thought that a time would come when I would describe something as existential as having a family, I was not prepared and so I faltered in my description. Yet Napoleon was patient, never interrupting. I told him about my father and mother, my siblings and their friends that they brought home, some of whom got my mother riled up. When I got to the point where my mother would always get us up to pray every morning and how I so hated the disturbance, he laughed so hard that I thought I had said something out of line.

"Why are you laughing?" I asked in wonder.

"So you don't think it is funny?" he asked.

"What do you mean? It is not funny."

"But you said you would be sleeping while clapping."

"Yes, it is very serious. I hated my house because every morning we are expected to pray. And you know how sweet sleep could be at that time of the morning."

I went on to talk about the many quarrels I had with my siblings, the fights and the curses. And then there was my father who would always keep to himself and whose voice was hardly to be heard. My description ended when I got to the day of the earthquake, and we fell silent.

"At least you have experienced it," he said.

"I wish I could have it back just the way that it was."

Three days later, a surprised Napoleon was called again to Madame Beaumont's office. The morning dragged into evening, and Napoleon never returned. He had been adopted and so had left the orphanage.

EIGHTEEN

Avan ou monte bwa, gade si ou ka desann li

Before climbing up a tree, see if you can climb it down, we always say.

Dr Chukwuemeka came to the police station.

He said he had been contacted by the university and so had come straight away. He talked with the policemen, answered their questions and made some calls.

There was no telling who it was, but I could only guess that it must have to be someone at the university.

They made him sign some papers and then I was allowed to go with him. It was to his house we went, and even though it was a walking distance, yet he had taken a taxi.

"You have had your first taste of the system," he said lightly, as he handed me a beer and then settled into a sofa. He popped the cork on a bottle of beer and took a generous swig.

"I am sorry for the inconvenience, Prof."

"No. I am the one who owes you an apology. I never knew that giving you my access card could be problematic."

"I also don't think it should. For a moment, I feared I would be charged with terrorism considering the way they handled the issue. The security man should simply have turned me away or confiscated the access card instead of involving the police."

"Don't worry about that. It is over now."

"So how will you get back the access card? I hope it won't cause you any troubles?"

"The authorities are sounding like they would give me a bit of a hard time for giving another person my access card. But never mind, the situation is nothing that a jovial smile won't take care of."

"Thank you, Prof."

"No need."

We drank our beers in silence.

"Did you get the news?"

"What news?" he asked.

"My president was assassinated."

He regarded me with a look of contained incredulity. "When did this happen?"

"I saw the news on the TV while I was in the police station. They said he was brutally murdered in his house and his wife is being taken into medical care due to the experience."

Dr. Chukwuemeka let down his beer. I could tell that he was mortified by the news.

"Who could be behind this thing?" he asked no one in particular.

"It could be anybody," I said. "I am sure that there would be a lot of speculations now. My country has enemies, and these are people who will want to keep the country poor."

"Hmmm," Dr Chukwuemeka said, gently pulling onto his beard - a gesture that depicted that he was lost in thought.

"We have enemies from within. Oligarchs. They serve the interests of enemies from without. And the present narrative of the country is what they want to maintain ... but how could they? This is too brazen. How could they have had the temerity to murder President Moise, a serving president of a country?"

"What kind of man was he? I mean your President."

"He had plans. A lot of people wanted him out. There were many protests ... but he was a good man, I think. They shouldn't have murdered him. It is an insult to the country … to everybody … it is an insult … barbaric … very wrong on every side."

"I am sure the international community will do something about it."

"You think so?"

"For their own good, yes. It would look bad that the serving president of a UN member state would be murdered, and nothing would come out of it. But on the second thought I think I should share a bit in your skepticism. You folks are of African descent after all, and where it concerns Africans, it becomes expedient that the rules do not apply any longer. We have seen it happen a good number of times and nothing has changed at the end of each one of them. It is always the same thing playing over and over again." He shook his head. "Dear me! Now I am worried."

NINETEEN

Sa pòv genyen se li I bay pitit li

We all know that what the poor has, is what he gives to his child.

Whenever I told the story of Napoleon and the days that followed in the orphanage, it was usually the case that my listeners felt a reliving of the pain and it surprised me that like a snail and its shell, I was carrying some weight with such deftness, which would allow me to share a part of it whilst not allowing anyone to partake in the weight.

It was Dr Chukwuemeka who told me that I bore a burden that I had not healed from.

Napoleon's adoption left me feeling like I had been

hollowed out and the part of me left for others to see was nothing short of an apparition propped up only by everything that echoed within me.

And the things that echoed were not pleasant. It showed in the manner in which I was being treated and in which I treated others. The other boys began to complain that I had become aggressive. I got into fights many times until I had exhausted Madame Beaumont and her repeated warnings.

Truly, in all of those times I had never been the aggressor. I was no longer respecting the established underground peck order amongst us boys; I could not continue walking about with my head bowed, avoiding eye contact and allowing others take first pass before me. I no longer allowing any of that, and because of this, some big boy would always pick offense and I would be ready to return the first punch thrown at me with more than just a clenched fist.

Once, I had slammed an iron bucket into a boy's face and for that I was put in solitary confinement for two weeks as though I was a prisoner.

When I came out of solitary confinement, most of the boys gave me a wide berth. I was considered dangerous and the quietness that I had acquired in the two weeks I had been all by myself helped all the more to lend me that mystical aura of the hardest of men.

Needless to say, the fieriness inside of me reflected itself in my phenotype; my eyes became sunken, and I had somewhat of a stoop around my shoulders. I could see notice it whenever my eyes darted to the mirror in the communal bathroom, and I hated what I saw.

I hated the mirror for being there, and reminding me of the stranger I had become, and it must have been this hatred directed at the poor mirror that had seen so many orphaned boys come and go that made me smash a boy's head into it. The unfortunate fellow - for truly, he was of the most unfortunate kind - had asked all the smaller boys to leave the bathroom as himself and his team of five would want to use it. The smaller boys had scampered away, naked, and all lathered up.

I had defied him and his team and went on washing in myself in the steamy shower. All five of them had looked on, at a loss for how to put me in my place. Ignoring them, I had finished off and went to the area for brushing my teeth. Every now and then, my gaze wandered to the mirror, but I would look away. The sight of me never impressed me anymore and because of that I always hastened with my business about that corner of the bathroom. I would have hurried over and got done with my business as usual had the five boys not hurried towards me, with the unfortunate one who obviously was their leader walking up ahead of the pack.

"You think you can keep on disrespecting everyone here you black monkey?" he said in his accent that sounded as though he was speaking through his nostrils. "Go back to the jungle where …"

I had not allowed him to finish. But in a flash, I grabbed him in a choke hold and, pushing him with every strength in me, rammed him towards the mirror where the back of his head smashed against it. When I let go of him, he crumbled to the floor, feeling around his head. The sight of his own blood frightened him so much that he went into hysteria. His friends, mortified with disbelief at the unexpected turn of events, hurried him away in the direction of the infirmary.

I thought I would be summoned to Madame Beaumont's office, but the whole day pass and there was no summons. Everyone stayed away from my path. They must have thought me a vicious animal. The next day passed, and still nothing from Madame Beaumont, and on the third day, just as I was beginning to think that it was either Madame Beaumont had not heard of the incidence or out of sheer helplessness over the situation had decided to pay it deaf ears, the summons came.

Madame Beaumont was with a priest when I stepped into her office. His black cassock hung on his frame as though it was not made for him. Behind his thick glasses, were sunken eyes that told of a life devoted to studies and piety. His thinning hair and general demeanour told of a man who cared for very little in life.

"This is Father Anthony," Madame Beaumont said to me in a manner that was too civil as to be considered unnecessary considering the trouble that I was causing her. "He is your new guardian. You will go with him."

“Where to?” I asked.

“Where he takes you to,” she said. “As long as he is taking you very far away from this place, I am fine with it, and you must follow him!”

There wasn’t much more for me to have said. I had never seen Madame Beaumont, ever so collected and reserved, lose her calm as she did on that afternoon. I remained quiet where I stood, waiting for a cue that would dictate for me the next thing that was expected of me.

“What do they call you?” the priest asked in a voice that was so strained that it appeared to be barely above a whisper.

“Claude … Claude, sir.”

“Good. Now come, Claude.”

CHAPTER TWENTY

Ti chen gen fòs devan kay mèt li

A small dog is brave in front of its master's house.

Father Anthony was English.

And just as I deduced, he was a man who studied a lot and hardly spoke. Possibly it was usual for him to forget his own voice.

That afternoon, he had taken me to his home in Normandy, an old mansion that overlooked the sea in the far distance. The house was huge, and it was a wonder that he lived all alone in it. An old lady came twice every week to clean the place and there was a gardener who came now and then to tend to the lawns and flowers. The house was spartan.

Nothing about it suggested luxury. The furnishing was bare, having only essentials. What the house had in abundance was books and silence - lots of them. Everywhere one turned, there were shelves of books, most of which spanned the entire walls, often reaching to the ceiling. Even in the toilets, there were books to be found there.

I had thought Father Anthony to be a priest, but he headed no church and often had visitors, fellow priests come to spend time with him in which they would discuss at length in low tones over tea or coffee and they would purr over volumes. Sometimes they prayed and meditated and would never care if I existed. Father Anthony never talked to me either.

He gave me no rules. Soon as we arrived he had led me into the house and showed me the room that I was to be sleeping in. It had a single bed and window that overlooked the garden at the back of the house. But then for walls, it had shelves of books.

There were piles and piles of books on the floor too, so that I could not move freely if I was not to bump a toe against any of the piles. After then, if I were to see Father Anthony, it would have to be in his study on the upper floor. And he left the huge door open, but I would never have the presence of mind to interrupt him seeing how he was hunched over some volume, reading and only stopping to make notes in one of the little books he always carried around somewhere within the folds of his cassock.

It was the cleaning lady that helped me out of the dilemma that was my new home. She had nearly had a heart attack when she had suddenly looked up from her cleaning one morning to see me. Apologizing, I had introduced myself.

"You are the unfortunate child that Father Anthony was going to pick up at the orphanage?" she had asked.

I didn't know how to respond as I wouldn't know which I would be agreeing to; whether the part about being unfortunate or the part about coming from the orphanage. "I never knew he was going to bring a black boy. Poor Father Anthony! God bless his kind soul. Come, let me show you about the house so you don't get in Father Anthony's way and condemn his kind heart to endless worries."

The cleaning lady, her name was Elyna, she turned out not to be the snob that she had initially impressed upon me. After getting over the initial shock of coming to close proximity to an African - she had told me that I was the closest she had ever been to one - she had turned out a likeable woman. A grandmother who had suffered a bad marriage and who lived all by herself some distance away, she showed me about the house and taught me how to look after myself.

"Father Anthony wouldn't be able to take care of himself, so you must not expect him to look out for you. It is he who needs your help and not the other way round," she had told me.

I learned from her that Father Anthony was a very important man, a close friend to the Pope, but who was dedicated more than anything to a life of studies. She thought me how to make coffee and tea just as Father Anthony liked and then to take it to him in his study, leave it at a designated table without bothering the man. I got along fine with Elyna. Whenever she didn't have any cleaning to do, we talked. She asked a lot of questions about me and where I come from. She asked to know what it meant for my skin to be melanated and if I felt any different in my skin. It didn't strike me as surprising that she had never heard of Haiti, and it confounded her that it wasn't some other obscure village in Africa.

"But I thought all black people live in Africa?"

"You have never heard of Jamaica, Trinidad and Tobago or St Lucia?"

She shook her head and said that if she had money she would travel to see the world and that it made her ashamed seeing that there was so much to the world's people that she was too ignorant about. I began to look forward each time to her visit, and when she came she brought me gifts of pastries and other things she cooked. Sometimes she brought berries and grapes. Whenever she was not around, I would be all by myself in the house. The gardener was not much of a company as he was deaf in both ears. But he had a habit of treating me to his warm smiles and nodding at me when I waved. Other than that, our paths never crossed.

With so much of free time in the absence of Elyna, I began to explore the most prominent aspect of the house - the books. I began from the ones in my bedroom, flipping through the cover pages and seeing what they were about. They were mostly books on geography, history and religion and a few on literature.

And from the look of them, they had been collected from the rarest of sources. Something told me that the books are the kind that could not be gotten just anywhere. And it was this sense of rarity that drew me into opening the first of them, to read from its pages, for even though most of them were in English, but there were some in French, Spanish and German and all the languages which Father Anthony was conversant with.

TWENTY-ONE

Sa ki pa touye ou, li angrese ou

My grandmother, whom I haven't really talked about, once said: "What does not kill you, fattens you!"

In the home of Father Anthony, I began my romance with books.

Books, I was soon to discover, held in them the magic to transport a reader to worlds that exist far from their reach; worlds created by the magic of worlds and trapped and bound in the letters imprinted on the paper pages which, although appearing inanimate, were very much alive.

With all the quietness and seclusion which my new home afforded me, I had all the time and privilege to soak in as much as my new taste for the pleasures of reading dictated.

One day, I went about getting Father Anthony some tea. I had taken it up to him in his study, placed the jar of tea in its place and would have snuck away as quietly as I had come in had I not thought that he mentioned my name. His voice was too unfamiliar about the house that when he spoke, one had to be sure that they heard correctly.

"Claude," he called me a second time, and I turned around to see him looking at me. He had led down his spectacles and I was seeing his eyes for about the first time. They were so sunken deep in their sockets that they appeared to be two dots on his face. I came over to him. "Please sit," he said, gesturing at a deep sofa a few metres to his right where he usually sat sometimes, especially when the reading was a light one.

I obliged him, settling into the sofa, conscious that I was taking up a hallowed spot in the study.

"What do you think of the world in its present state?" Father Anthony had asked me.

I willed myself to speak even as it struck me that I might risk not saying the right thing. "The world, Father," I managed to bring myself to say, "is filled with many troubles."

He fell silent, pondering what I had said. I knew that what I had said was as shallow as it was stupid. It was a generalization aimed at hiding its lack of substance, but Father Anthony was giving it too much importance in thinking about it. This got me all the more uncomfortable.

"Have you been able to sample any of the books in this house?"

For a moment, I thought to lie, not knowing if the fact that I was reading his books was to be considered an offense. Elyna never read them, neither did the gardener, and I had never had the presence of mind to enquire from Elyna if reading Father Anthony's books was to be considered an offense.

"I have, father."

"Good. Very good," he muttered, and then looking up at me. "Books are good for the mind. You should indulge in them as much as you can."

Elated, I nodded and then he waved me away and returned his attention to the leather bound volumes that lay opened before him.

I think Father Anthony was pleased with me that I had begun to read his books, and I was pleased with myself because since came to France I started to gain someone's approval.

The encounter in the study, if anything, gave me a morale boost that saw me move about the house with more confidence. I read more of the books and soon I had consumed up most of the books in my room except for the ones on early navigation which I considered too complex for my tastes.

With the books in my room done with, I began to venture onto the shelves about the house.

It was books of literature that I preferred the most, and of those ones there were more of historical fiction. I would read from morning, often skipping meals and most of the time dozing off when my mind had gotten exhausted from the endless journeys and adventures I subjected it to.

Elyna began to take notice of my newfound habit.

I no longer was available to have discussions with her when she came around to clean the house. Gone were those moments when I looked forward to her coming with great expectations. If for anything, I became indifferent to her comings and goings. Soon, she complained.

She said I was becoming very much like Father Anthony and that it was possible that we were both cut from the same cloth after all. In time she began to pay me no mind. She would come around, go about her task of cleaning up the house and would leave without getting in my way or in the way of Father Anthony. We became for her the two masters of the mansion who were meant not to be seen or bothered.

Days later, I had gone up to the study to serve tea when Father Anthony called my attention again as like the last time.

"What do you think of the world?" he asked.

"I think the world is a place driven by the thought and desires of people with ambition and sustained by people without it."

"Hmmm," he said, and stroked his bare chin. "And have you given thoughts about your place in it?"

"I think I will prefer to be a man who has a choice in the affairs of his own world."

"And how do you intend to do that?" he asked.

"I am learning from you."

"How so?"

I braced up for what I feared would be a long lecture on my part and also an attempt to impress my benefactor, all the while fearing that something could go wrong, and I would end up with the opposite result.

"It is said that we are drawn and tempted by our desires. Out there, there are many men who wake up at sunrise to labour at some job that they detest so much, but because they have desires and obligations to meet, they have no option than to sell a part of their time and peace to work in a manner that ambitious men have carved out for them. But with you, it is different.

You don't have the same ambitions as other men, and this means that you have all aspect of your life to yourself. You freely devote every aspect of your life to the one thing that you love to do. Nobody has claimed to any part of you. You are contributing to the world on your own terms.

My father, when he was alive was a civil servant. I don't think he liked his job. It put him under constant stress, and he was always happy to escape from it at the end of each day. Yet in the morning, he would drag himself to go labour at it. I think such a life makes people get old too soon but because they have to pay for rent and pay off their loans, feed their families and meet other obligations, they have very few options. But with you, I can see that you work harder and longer than my father and you love the work you do. It is your life. That is how I want to live mine."

Father Anthony regarded me intently by the time I had finished. I feared that I might not have made any sense, and that I sounded naive. Maybe he would see through what I had done - that I had merely gone in circles, repeating myself over and over in a bid to somehow make a desperate jab at arriving at a sensible conclusion.

"Are you saying that you will want to become a priest just like me?"

"No, Father. I will not want to be a priest, I am afraid. I may not be able to meet with the demands of priesthood, but I will want to be a free man, free enough to pursue the things that I find most interesting in life."

"So tell me, what will you want to pursue in life?"

"I want to become the president of my country someday. I want to make my country known and respected all over the world."

"That is a noble undertaking, my son. But then you must first have to understand the world completely. The world is both complex and simple and you will have to familiarize yourself with all of these parts. And most importantly you must have to make friends in powerful places."

"How do I make powerful friends?" I asked.

"To do that you must first have to understand every aspect of the world and every of its peoples. This is the reason countries have envoys and embassies in other countries. I am sure you know what that is."

"Yes," I said.

"Good. You will have to understand the world's peoples so you can relate with them from the position of their need. And then, as I mentioned, you will have to make friends amongst them. You are a young man and a bright one at that. The easiest way for you to befriend future leaders from different nations is to go the one of the top universities where they all come together to study."

"Oxford," I said. "My father used to say that I will study in Oxford. He said that that was where I was sure to get the best education that would guarantee them a place in the future. He wanted me to be a minister of my country someday. It was his dream that I go to Oxford."

"Yes, and there is Harvard and Yale in the United States. They are all elite schools. The kind of places you go to make friends and secure for yourself connections that may come in handy."

"But they are expensive."

"Ambition is always expensive, my son. You will have to figure out a way to pay for it. It is the way of the world, and you will have to understand the aspect of its complexity."

Our discussion left me wondering how it was possible that I could get into Oxford - or Yale or Harvard as Father Anthony had mentioned. Sometimes I dreamed of it, that I was already in Oxford, studying.

I dug around for information, to realise that it was not an easy thing to get into Oxford, and it cost a lot.

It was the cost that got me anxious.

But Father Anthony had mentioned that I would have to figure out a way to pay my way into Oxford.

Was he simply generalising, or did he think that somehow an orphaned boy from Haiti could pull a stunt and get himself into Oxford?

What was it about me that I could pay with? I thought about these for many days until the idea began to fade away from my consciousness out of weariness because I had exhausted every possibility that I could think of as a means to getting into Oxford. In time I ditched the idea and sought solace instead in the books in Father Anthony's house.

We are drawn by our desires.

Was I not the one who said that to Father Anthony? Hence I decided to let the matter of Oxford rest.

I read as much as I could, reading up many of the works in French and then I began to practise reading in English.

TWENTY-TWO

Se aprè batay ou konte blese

It is after the battle that we count the wounded.

I have heard it said many times.

And also, I have heard many times that the only thing constant in life is change. And this phenomenon is generally expressed in every facet of life and in everything that bears a hint of life in it.

It is seen in the skies, as the clouds are in constant motion, gathering and dispersing to give way to rainfall and shine. The trees say as much too; blossoming today and shedding their foliage tomorrow as the seasons dictate. It is seen in man and woman; as childhood comes in the morning and grows into old age at dusk.

Yet not all change is welcome, especially in the world of humans, for we always have preference for one stage of life over the other. However, irrespective of whether or not we like it, like everything else that is in contact with life and the living, we must have to bear witness to change and take part in it.

A lot of changes had come upon my life, sudden changes, and they had happened up until my arrival at Father Anthony's house.

At that point, I thought I would prefer things to remain as they were even though I knew that with the little times I discussed with Father Anthony, there would have to be a future to look forward to.

Yet I was afraid. I was afraid of changes, of a time when I would have to do things differently and be treated by things differently; I feared a time when I would have to step into unfamiliar terrains and begin yet again to adjust to the things that I was not used to.

I wanted no changes, nothing different from the peace and quiet of Father Anthony's mansion and the assurances that every day would be like the one before it, and the one after it, and that no day dawned upon me with any surprises lurking in the corner.

But then all of these were the flimsy wishes of one mortal upon the grand workings of the universe which went on grinding, slowly but surely, paying no heed to the futile wishful rebellions of human specks willing to turn it this way or that as suits their conflicting whims.

Change came for me in the form of a visit.

It was a woman. She called upon the mansion late one rainy evening.

And although she was weary and dressed as one who had been on the road for many days, yet her state as it were could not hide the last vestige of beauty that was leaving with fading youth.

It was Elyna who had answered the door - for it was one of those days when she was about the house doing the cleaning that needed to be done.

I for my part was privileged at the time to be lounging on a seat in the sitting room, fatigued from reading and almost drifting into slumber until the knock had jolted me awake.

Before the visitor could state her business, recognition came over Elyna, and like one intent on hiding a secret, she spirited the woman into the house and out of view of any prying neighbour - not that they were any, for the mansion, as I had mentioned, was on a secluded piece of land that looked out to the sea in the far distance. Elyna took the lady to one of the rooms and I could see her hurry towards the study, apparently to summon Father Francis.

By this time every form of fatigue had cleared from my mind as I suspected that something had to be amiss.

Yet I was at a loss for what to do as it was clear from the look of things that whatever it was that was playing out of the house must mean to be no business of mine and I would be intruding if I tried to learn what it was about. For the rest of the day there was a certain disquiet that held sway over the house.

Father Anthony left his study and never returned to it, and when he did leave the room where the strange woman had been put up, it was to attend to one thing or another in one part of the house and he did it with a sense urgency that hinted to the fact that all was not well.

As for Elyna, she hardly ever left the strange woman's room and when night came she never returned to her place as she was wont to. I observed all of this while staying out of everyone's way. And they went about their hushed affairs as though I had ceased to exist in their consciousness.

You could imagine the state of my wonder even as left to myself I attributed many possible scenarios to the event that was playing out.

I was a young man left to himself and his imagination running wild as he tried to piece together the fragments of the events playing out, with him as the sole deprived spectator.

Whenever either Father Anthony or Elyna left the room, I would peer and look intently at the one in a bid to pick up any hint of information that their demeanour would possibly give away.

But all that I could guess from them were exactly nothing to go by and therefore I was left to myself and my thoughts - poor me, confused, perplexed, unsure of what the coming of the woman and the effect it had on everyone else would bode for me.

At the stroke of midnight unsure of what to expect any longer, I returned to my room. But sleep eluded me. I tossed about in my bed, restless. In my books, there was no succour to be found either. I would gaze at the pages of the books, but my mind registered nothing. Restless, I tossed the book and listened for anything that might hint as to the goings-on about the house, but the walls were such that were thick, and nothing escaped from one room to the next that wasn't short of an explosion. With that level of restlessness and uncertainty I resigned myself to a night that would appear to be one of the longest of my life.

How I was able to fall asleep remained something of a mystery to me. But I had woken up late the next morning unsure of what to look forward to.

The house was quiet as I stepped out of my room, and unusually so. In the kitchen I walked into Elyna cooking.

There was a certain stiffness about her frame and there was nothing about her usual cheer. She only muttered her acknowledgement of my greeting. From the look of things, she had spent the night at the house and had not returned to her house.

"Elyna," I said, unsure whether I was doing the

right thing in prying. "What is happening? Who is that woman?"

She paused from stirring the porridge in a pot, long enough to regard me with something that I suspected to be pity, or was it a struggle within her to come to terms with the realization that I had been in existence all the while, even though I had been forgotten.

"Father Anthony will explain to you when he is ready."

"Don't you want to tell me?" I pressed.

"No."

"But is everything okay? Because I don't think so."

"I told you not to worry. Father Anthony will explain to you if he wants to."

"Okay," I said. It was mostly because I wanted something else to say.

"And please, don't question him about this until he is ready. Best to keep away from him in the meantime. Do whatever you have to do, but don't get in his way."

TWENTY-THREE

Se lè koulèv mouri ou wè longè l

It is when the snake dies that we can see its length.

Father Anthony was ready to talk to me later that afternoon.

I had gone to send him tea in his study, but he was nowhere in his usual place when I walked in. Placing the jar of tea at its usual spot in the study, I turned to leave when I saw him standing at the door.

"I apologise for startling you," he said. And truly he had, for I had never seen the man look so pale and drawn. He likely must not have slept a whiff all night long, and his hair appeared ruffled. His eyes had a distant look to them that I had never recognized. "Please come with me," he said.

I followed him to the balcony, stopping to stand before him as he looked out to the sea in the distance. He drew air into his lungs and then exhaled. It was as though he was only remembering to breathe and was taking in as much air as he could now that it had occurred to him. For me, I stood there beside him, silent, pondering what it was he wants to disclose to me or question me about. With Father Anthony, there was no telling what was to be expected and he was very much an enigma.

"Is everything alright, Father?" I managed to ask.

"Who are we to say?" was his reply. I would have asked some more, but then I remembered that Elyna had warned me not to question Father Anthony on the events of the previous night. "I will be going away," Father Anthony said, looking out straight ahead.

"For how long, Father?"

He hissed. "For a long, long time," and then he turned to me. "You will be returning to your former home." The words hit the breath out of me, and I feared that I would crumble where I stood. But I didn't. How I managed to remain standing in my state of shock remains for me a surprise. Yet I was there, beside Father Anthony, the man who had become my sole benefactor for two months, listening to him tell me that the bubble I had lived in was about to burst. "A car will come to take you in an hour's time."

"Where are you going to?" I managed to ask in my dazed state.

"I will be going abroad. It is best for everyone that way."

"But Father, who is that woman who came yesterday? Is she the reason you are leaving?"

Father Anthony regarded me for a while. There was a sort of softness that had come over his eyes. I could feel in them the conflict that ran within his soul that I had known all the while to hold the sort of calmness that is not of this world. In all the time I had known him, never had I seen him in the state he was; vulnerable, ruffled, almost disoriented. I thought he would provide me with an answer and that he was struggling within himself undecided about what part of the truth he was to bother my young mind with, and what part of it he should hold back. But he didn't say anything. Instead, he patted my shoulder in the fondest of manners and then walked away, leaving me standing there, an effigy in the wind.

That evening when I was driven back into the familiar orphanage, I felt that I was a toy being returned by a customer to a store shelf, that my worth wasn't what it appeared to be, and that everyone would see that and treat me to less regard than I had been meted out with.

And it was as I had thought, for the other boys sniggered and jeered when I walked past. They made remarks about me that I didn't want to pay attention to.

As for Madame Beaumont, she was not happy to have me back. If she had her way, I reasoned, she would have me out in the streets and far away from her orphanage. That much was evident in her demeanour. But then I decided to simply exist and take everything as they came. There was no point dreaming or expecting anything to happen in a certain manner. Whatever comes, and however it does, I would go along with it, I concluded.

I had been able to leave with some of Father Anthony's books, and with his permission, of course.

He had also had the presence of mind to send me off with a note addressed to Madame Beaumont, to allow me to keep the books as my property.

I suspected he had said some other endearing words in the letter which I am sure Madame Beaumont didn't buy into - I could tell that from the sneer on her face as she read the letter in front of me in her office - yet she had allowed me to keep the books. And it was in the books that I found company. I would find any quiet spot to read whenever I was not doing any chores. That way I kept out of people's way and helped them to keep out of mine. In the two months that I had been away, I noticed that there were some new boys added to the lot and there were some of the old faces who were nowhere to be seen.

They might have been adopted, I reasoned. Yet I decided to not make that my business. I didn't care. I wasn't welcome in the orphanage and didn't want to, either. If I had my choice I would never be found anywhere within a hundred miles of the place. But while I was there, I hoped to remain detached from it and everything it portended. And it was a good thing that somehow my reputation for being dangerous was still very much alive in the orphanage.

TWENTY-FOUR

Premye so pa so

There were times when I woke up on my spring bed and subconsciously, I would think that I was still in Father Anthony's mansion.

But after some minutes, I would realise that I had not woken up the sea air and that there would be no rushing out to the balcony to witness the sun rise over the sea in the distance.

The first jump, they say, is not a jump.

Most of the time I thought about that night when that strange woman had come knocking on the door.

I imagined who she might be.

But no one provided me with any answers when

I asked. Elyna had remained quiet about it and had taken the liberty to warn me against asking to know the identity of the woman. Father Anthony on his part had remained hushed about the whole affair and was very much unwilling to breathe a word of it.

I dared to hazard a few guesses; firstly that it was possible that the woman was some secret mistress he kept, or he had kept, and she had somehow re-surfaced; it was also possible that the woman had a child for him and had come up from the shadows of his past with some demands. It would not be out of place to think so as at that time I had already begun to hear news of priests keeping mistresses and having families in secret.

But what if the woman was none of these to him, but was something else more sinister and darker? Little wonder he was leaving abroad so soon. And what for? The more I tried to fathom the events of the past days that had rocked my world as I knew it, the more complex it seemed to me. And to think of Elyna, that she was in on whatever it was that had played out back there left me more confused. I began to think that she was more than a cleaning lady to Father Anthony.

She definitely was much more to him, more than I had thought until the coming of the strange woman. It bothered me that I would never know what it was that had transpired back there and who exactly Father Anthony was.

The only person whom I suspected would be able

to provide some clarity to the confusion that beset my mind would be none other than Madame Beaumont. But then, how could I have walked up to her, a woman who would wish me away if she could, with such questions.

Two months after my return to the orphanage, much of which had dragged on that it had looked like two centuries, I was summoned yet again to Madame Beaumont's office. There was a man in the office with her. He had the look of someone who spent a lot of time under the weather as much of his neck and his face were leathery and reddish pink. His arms as seen from his short sleeved shirt dampened with sweat, had he been older, would have been muscular and taut, but what would have been his muscle sagged beneath his wilted skin. Beside the man was a woman whom I thought to be his wife. Dressed in a bright floral gown and a hat, she looked an uneven pair with the man, for where he was collected and reserved, she looked like the kind who was outgoing and flashy. She was the one who spoke first and as soon as I had walked into the room.

"Is he the one you are talking about?" the man's wife asked, and without waiting for an answer, turned to her husband. "Benoit, he will do."

The husband, Benoit, nodded. It struck me then that he was the kind who would agree with her on anything;

a concession he must have learned to make over time, to maintain the peace.

"Claude," Madame Beaumont said to me. "This couple will be your new guardian. You will go with them, and they will take you to your new home."

I would have asked to know where my new home would be, but I didn't care at that point.

Not anymore.

Whatever took me away from the orphanage was a welcome development.

I listened to her with half a heart as she admonished me on the need to be of my best behaviour and to make sure that I wasn't returned otherwise I would have a hard time being accepted back. It sounded as though it was by any fault of mine that I was returned the first time from Father Anthony's house where, God knew, I would rather spend the rest of my life with - if I ever had any.

My new foster family - if that is what I should call them - was different from what I had previously had.

There were no books in the house, a poultry farm in the outskirts of a remote village miles and miles away from the orphanage.

Benoit, the man was a quiet kind, a strong man despite his age, who worked from sunrise to sundown and never seemed to have any issues with the long hours he worked. It was as though his life depended on it.

Sometimes I thought it was a ploy to get away from

his wife. Perhaps that had been the trick at the earliest stages, but then it had calcified into a habit which he lived out subconsciously as every time he was either lifting bags of chicken feed, sorting eggs, cleaning the battery cages or haggling with his suppliers and distributors. And as for his wife - Julia was her name - she would spend all day on the porch and only leaving to spend time in the beauty salon in town or to shop for groceries.

Apart from copies of the fashion magazines she bought every month, there were no books to be found about the house. Julia, I was soon to learn, had attained to some means from her previous divorce and had had two children with Benoit but they were studying in Paris, and never visited while I lived with the couple.

Monsieur Benoit taught me how to help out on the farm. At every sunrise I would find him already at work, toiling away. And there was always so much to do. While we worked, he would begin to talk to me, and these were mostly things about his life's experiences. I could tell that before my coming he had been bored and lacked someone to talk to, but with my coming he somehow hoped to relive his past in the telling of it.

"You know in my days; I was some very cool guy. I drove a truck, had the best girls. You should see me then."

We were taking a rest from cleaning the poultry house, and he had brought along a bottle of coke from which we poured into glass cups. "I used to spend a lot of time in the gym with my friends. It was such a good time."

I watched him look into space, momentary loss in thought as a broad smile played on his face. From the look of him, he had had a pleasant youth, just as he was telling me. That much was evident.

"Did you want to be a poultry farmer?" I asked. My question seemed to have jolted him back to the present.

"Who cared about the future then or what they would become when the future came around? We never bothered about those things. We simply went through life. The future was never a thing. They were always only the next day and the one after that."

I thought I understood him when he said so. His youthful days were no different from mine in that respect. Mine was as much as was never concerned with the future, as his. That outlook on life had been about to change when I lived with Father Anthony, but then I had been returned to the orphanage as though to remind me that I dared not think too seriously of myself as to attempt to look into the future and making plans for it. I was meant to live one day at a time, and never to look into the next day with any expectations. But then here was the difference between mine and Monsieur Benoit's youth; while he had it sunny, marked with exhilaration and youthful exuberance, mine was dull and bleak and had all the markings of misfortune and a most depressing form of uncertainty. There was nothing to look forward in it and any attempt to do so appeared like a form of rebellion punishable by an upheaval of a most traumatizing kind - the kind that followed after the appearance of the strange woman to Father Anthony's home.

"What about you?" he asked me. "Are there pleasant memories from where you come?"

I began to talk about the orphanage, but he stopped me, saying that he meant to hear about my country. It was quite surprising for me as the man had struck me as one who had no interest in anything that wasn't his birds.

"Yes, I have pleasant memories of Haiti," I told him. "I loved it there." And then I began to tell him about the lakes and waterfalls in my country, the beaches with their turquoise waters and white sand and coconut palms that lined the shores of the coasts lulling the senses to stretch beneath their shades and soak in the pleasure of the elements. He liked the things I said about my country, but I think he was having a hard time believing it.

"And your country is in Africa?"

"No. In the Caribbean." And then I went on to tell him how much in the Western Hemisphere we are, and about our relationship with the French. "That was how I came to speak French," I told him.

Monsieur Benoit nodded in understanding. He asked me about my family, the kind of foods we ate, and if the milk we drank in Haiti was mixed with charcoal to darken it. There was no offense to be detected in his questions, for I could tell that he was genuinely curious and didn't know any better. He told me that he once had an African classmate in school but that the one was French and didn't identify as anything else - neither as African or anything remotely connected to any other islands where Africans lived, and which wasn't to be found on the continent.

As for Madame Julia, Monsieur Benoit's wife, she didn't treat me with as much curiosity as her husband. But there were times when I suspected that she stared at me when she thought I wasn't noticing. She was one who stayed out of the day's business and never participated in our day's activities other than making sure that our meals where ready when we came into the house for lunch. And she was a good cook. But I could hear her chat away with her husband every night when they retired for bed. Oh, how noisy she was when the chats died away and made way for the creaks and moans that seemed to rock the house to its foundations. At those times, I learned to remain still and quiet in the small room allotted to me, never so much as stirring or making the slightest noise as to make my foster parents aware of my presence. It was best that I was totally forgotten at those hours, unholy or pleasurable as they might be.

TWENTY-FIVE

Nen pran kou; je kouri dlo

Dr. Chukwuemeka returned with me to the police station the next day, but it did not turn out as I had feared.

We were not kept long.

He talked with an officer and then we both signed some papers and were allowed to go.

"I am asked to come to my faculty to pick up the access card," he told me as we departed the police station.

"I am sorry that I have caused you so much trouble," I said but then he waved me off.

"This kind of unforeseen things happen. It is nobody's fault."

"Will this be on my record or something?" I asked.

"I know how it usually is with this kind of people. They put it on record against your name for every slight thing you do that they find displeasing."

"Why do you worry so much?" he asked with an understanding smile. "You committed no offense or crime. This thing has been sorted out. If you care coming my way, I am going to the faculty to pick up the access card."

"Yes, I am going with you."

"Good."

When we descended the stairs, we found the Royal Car, waiting.

We had to walk across the road the board it. The cab driver, a young man with a scanty beard whose hair was gathered in a bun behind his head struck up a conversation almost immediately he had joined the traffic. He wanted to know if we were both students.

"I lecture here," Dr Chukwuemeka told him.

"University of Oxford or Oxford Brookes?"

"University of Oxford. I am with the African Studies Centre."

The man was impressed. He introduced himself as Rayan. His mother was Lithuanian and his father Pakistani. He had migrated to England three years ago and had completed a master's degree somewhere in London.

Dr Chukwuemeka spoke something to him in a strange tongue and the man was shocked.

"You speak Urdu?" he asked, and Dr Chukwuemeka said, "Yes."

He asked: "How come?"

"I lived in India when I was much younger." He continued. "I learnt Hindi. There's no much difference between Urdu and Hindi."

"Yes, I know," he responded.

The taxi driver was impressed.

"So, what took you to India?"

"I went there for studies, and it was there that I wrote my first novel."

"Wow. That is interesting. So how do you find India?"

"India is quite an interesting place, a place of contradictions. You see the rich and the abject poor living in close proximity to each other."

"That is one way of putting it."

For me, I kept to myself, listening in on the conversation between the two and gleaning as much as I could.

Dr Chukwuemeka had never told me about his days in India, and I suspected it was mostly because with me he was concerned about hearing my story than telling his. So with the conversation ongoing with the taxi driver, I saw my chance to listen and learn as much as I could.

The conversation veered off India, into Pakistan, Iraq and then the Western countries.

They discussed archaeological and historical evidence to the development of cultures in that region of the world even as they got influenced by Western contacts.

At last we arrived at our destination, which was Heat African Restaurant on Cowley Road and bade goodbyes.

"I have been to many countries in the world," Dr Chukwuemeka said. "And in none of them have I met cab drivers as informed as the ones you find in Oxford."

Getting back the access card was the easiest part of the entire series of events involved with putting the matter to rest.

The receptionist at the faculty, on recognizing Dr Chukwuemeka smiled, greeted him warmly and handed him the access card.

She politely asked that he signed into a ledger, and then that was it.

We had gone there before the restaurant.

"You see? No need to worry yourself that much," he said to me as we walked away from the faculty.

"I was afraid that I was causing you a lot of inconvenience and I didn't want it prolonged."

"Were you afraid that you could cause Monsieur Benoit any inconveniences in the while you were living with him?"

I mused over the thought. No answer that I could come up with seemed definitive enough.

"I think there were times when I was conscious of

getting in the way of anything. In fact most of the time I was conscious of making any mistakes. I didn't want to be returned to the orphanage."

"Was that so?"

"Yes. There were times when I was worried that I had actually gotten in the way of things, though."

"Tell me about it."

I told Dr Chukwuemeka about the day that I had gotten in the way of things in Monsieur Benoit's household.

At least that was what I thought - that I had gotten in the way of things. It had happened one afternoon when Monsieur Benoit had gone into town and left me in charge of things at home.

I think he had gone to settle some misunderstanding with a supplier, and which had something to do with a payment that had delayed in coming.

Madame Julia who had left much earlier in the day returned shortly afterwards. He had company in the form of a woman about her own age. I saw them pull at the driveway and then Madame Julia in the company of the woman had walked towards the farm to enquire about her husband. When I told her where he had gone to, she seemed disappointed, but then she returned to the house with her visitor, and I paid no more mind to it all.

I had worked until high noon when I needed something chilled to drink. It was at that time when

Monsieur Benoit would go for a beer and would invite me to take a glass. But since he was not around, I felt it sinful to indulge alone. So as I approached the house, I made up my mind that I would settle for either water or any of those freshly pressed fruit juices which Madame Julia used to make.

I had gone into the house when I chanced upon Madame Julia and her friend in the sitting room in a position which I found most awkward. They seemed to be inclined towards each other on the couch and at angles that startled me. It was the fact that each woman was without her clothes that jolted me. For a moment, I stood, frozen, unable to move a limb as my mind appeared to have left me. I have heard about these things, but like a child who might have been privy to information way above their age but yet unprepared for the moment when they would walk in on adults in the very act that they had gossiped, theorized and often joked about. It was the visitor who first spotted me for she was the one who had her line of view towards the door where I stood momentarily transfixed.

My presence got her startled and she jumped to collect herself. Madame Julia, on noticing the object of her friend's sudden reaction, began to placate her.

"I thought you said there was no one around? He nearly gave me a heart attack."

"Don't worry. He is just a boy. A foster child."

"I thought it was a burglar."

"No," she said, and then turning to me: "What do you want? Are you planning on standing there all day to become a spectator?"

"Sorry," I began, wondering how come my throat had gone so suddenly dry that it hurt to talk. "I was actually going to the refrigerator."

"Then get along! Stop acting weird. You are making my visitor uncomfortable."

I had tried to forget about that day, but I never thought that Madame Julia did forget it.

The next day she had told me that she never wanted me to breathe a word of what I had seen but I was too shocked to say anything for never had I seen her as ferocious as that day.

But she never let it be at that.

She never was her former self in the days that followed for it appeared I had become for her a subject of interest; not the kind that you would expect, but of a more toxic kind that anyone in my situation would never wish for.

For everything I did, she found fault in. And I found myself unable to stay away from her path any longer for the more I tried to do so, she found ways to get me in the way of her disapproval.

Luckily Monsieur Benoit never took her complaints to heart. Instead he would grunt his replies and nod his head in response to her complaints to the extent that sometimes I thought he was somehow low in the head.

One of such times, she had told him that she thought I could seek work elsewhere rather than in the household, to which he nodded as he was wont to.

"But you have to say something or better still do something about this. Where do you stand with my suggestion?"

"Cherie, but he helps with the work around the house. He is helpful."

"Yet he has to grow into his own man at some point. Don't you think so?"

"I will think about it."

"No you won't! I am sure of that!!"

"Cherie?" he called after, confused for her outburst while she stormed away from him and bounded up the stairs to their room.

From where I stood by the doorway that led into the kitchen I watched the events play out, unseen.

Monsieur Benoit remained silent after his wife had stormed away, but that was for a moment, for then he let out a heavy sigh and continued from where he had left off with his eating. I felt pity for him.

That night, I could hear Madame Julia shout at him and scream her frustrations but there was not a word to be heard from him. A door slammed shut too loudly and then there was total silence.

For much of the night, I stayed awake thinking.

Fear gripped me. It was the same fear that had come over me a few months before when I had been told that I would be leaving Father Anthony's house for the orphanage.

There were times when I toyed with the idea of running away, to wherever it was as long it took me out of sight and away from the continuous displeasure that Madame Julia had come to develop for me.

I would imagine packing my books and my other belongings - which amounted to the clothes and a pair of shoes that I had come to possess in the while I had moved in with Monsieur Benoit and his wife - into a rucksack and disappearing.

I had no money and had seen no need for it, and this was my greatest worry. To run away from the home, I reasoned that I would need money, at least for a bus ride. I would run far away to Paris.

Paris was a big city, my dream city and there I could find people who looked like me. There, I reasoned, I would get a job and decide for myself what next to do with my life.

But then I remembered yet again that I had no money.

What if I asked Monsieur Benoit for money? The idea didn't seem right enough. He would begin to ask me what I needed the money for, and I wouldn't know what to say to him. What if I stole some money? The idea didn't sit well with me. Besides I had no idea where to lay hands on money to make away with. It had never occurred to me to know where the household kept their money or whether they kept any money in the house.

But what if I stole any of Madame Julia's jewelry. It was possible that I could get somewhere to pawn it. In Paris, perhaps. But then, I would need money to get to Paris. And Paris, from my calculations, was a long way from Monsieur Benoit's house.

The more I thought about running away, the more the impossibility of the idea stared me in the face, but then Madame Julia never let down on her displeasure of me. If anything the passing of day emboldened it.

I didn't quite understand why she needed me out of her way. Was she afraid that I would let Monsieur Benoit or anyone else in on what I had chanced upon? But would Monsieur Benoit care about it were he to learn of it? I doubted.

The man went through life unbothered, and I wondered if anything would bother him. Perhaps if I were to run away, it might bother him, but I wondered for how long he would bear the burden before shrugging it on and plowing on with life as he knew and lived it.

Something happened soon enough that changed things for me. It happened in the form of an accident.

Monsieur Benoit had ridden to town in his truck and was taking too long to return. I was beginning to get worried, but I dared not go in the house to enquire from

Madame Julia for it seemed a bad idea to seek any form of confrontation with her.

A police car pulled in front of the house, and I watched with keen interest as they walked up to the front door and knocked. From the farm I watched them talk with Madame Julia and then together they rode away with a distraught Madame Julia.

This didn't help the state of my mind any bit for I ran many possibilities through my head. I didn't want to think about the most probable worst case scenario. There was no way I could bring myself to consider. The reality would be too harsh, and I was not ready to bear that possibility. So as the hours dragged by, my state of restlessness mounted.

It was not until the next day that Madame Julia returned to the house. She was barely recognizable for I had never seen her as disheveled as she was when she knocked on the door of my room. There was none of the acrimony which she had meted out to me in the past weeks. Her eyes were reddened and sunken and told of a night passed in tears. My heart sunk at the sight of her.

"What is the matter?" I asked.

She began to cry. "It is my husband."

"What … what happened … is he …"

"He had an accident. A car accident."

TWENTY-SIX

Ravèt pa janm gen rezon devan poul

A cockroach is never right in front of a chicken.

I later learnt of the details of what had happened.

Monsieur Benoit had had an accident.

When going to town he had tried to avoid hitting a deer that had suddenly scampered across the road, but he had swerved too sharply to steer the car back on the road. And it being a bend, he had skidded off the road and had the hit the car against the trunk of a tree. The doctors said it would take a long time before he would be able to return to home, but they were not sure if he would be able to make use of his legs in a long time.

"I think this is my body's way of telling me that it is

time to retire from active work," Monsieur Benoit had said jokingly from his hospital bed when I had gone to see him days after. He was a sorry sight, and I couldn't stand the thought of him swaddled up in bandages and having IV fluids sticking out his arm. He looked so vulnerable and prone for a man whom I had known to labour tirelessly for hours on end on his farm. And even though he tried to make light of the situation, yet I wasn't any comfortable. I bit back the tears that threatened to betray my feelings, but Monsieur Benoit had read through me. As for Madame Julia, she would not stop crying and appearing hysterical.

Every day, I would go to the hospital to spend at least an hour at his bedside. There wasn't much I could do. The nurses were kind and they tended him pretty well. But I felt it right to make out time each day to stay by the side of the one man by whose side I had learned to stay and with whom I had laboured through the heat and suffocation of the poultry farm every day. Sometimes when I arrived at his ward, there would be people, visitors with him. I had never known Monsieur Benoit to have a lot of friends, but it was becoming quite normal to find him in the company of people who most of the times brought baskets of or bouquet of flowers. On one of those days I had met him with just one man, a burly fellow who looked more German than French.

"This is Monsieur Wolfgang. He is my friend," Monsieur Benoit made the introduction. The man simply nodded to me and gave me a smile. “I can’t continue with the farm, Claude. You already know the situation of things. You have heard what the doctors have said. And I know that you alone can’t handle the affairs of the farm. Therefore I have sold the farm to Monsieur Wolfgang. But what about you? What are your plans?”

“I … I don’t know.”

“Monsieur Wolfgang will hire you as one of his workers if you want. I have sold the house too and will be moving away to Lyon with my wife. Some of my family live there. It is better for me to spend the rest of my life close to them.”

Even though I didn’t like the thought of the poultry and house coming under the ownership of anyone else, I agreed to work for the new owner, Monsieur Wolfgang. I didn’t know what my pay would amount to, and he didn’t mention it. Perhaps we would talk about it later so that I could know what I would be looking forward to at the end of every month. And I promised myself to save as much as I would; for this, I perceived, was a sign that I would eventually be moving to Paris.

The new owner, Monsieur Wolfgang, resumed ownership of the farm a week later. But rather than come in person, he had a representative come in his stead. The man, tall, slender man with a pencil moustache moved in with eight others young men who were to be workers on the farm.

Mr. Klaus was his name - the man. As for his workers' names, I had a way of mixing them up and so I feared that I would soon give up on the attempt of knowing who he was amongst all. Mr. Klaus seemed to have an issue with me, I guess because of the colour of my skin and his obvious attitude was reflected in a lesser extent in the workers whom he had brought along like flies on the sore ears of a street dog. The workers, all eight of them, considered it demeaning to labour alongside me. They would sit back and allow me to do the bulk of the work while they conversed in German, made jokes, smoked and laughed.

Much of the time I felt that I was the subject of their laughter, but I told myself to pay them no mind. In this manner my new life dragged on, not one bit what I had envisioned nor wished for myself.

TWENTY – SEVEN

Se bon kè krapo ki fè l san tèt

Michael heard about what had happened at the Weston Library and was soon at my apartment.

"How did you know about this?" I asked him.

"How do you mean?" he fired back. "This happened at the Weston Library and not at some back alley. People saw it. They were talking about it. At first I thought it was some random happening that I was not meant to concern myself with until someone told me that it was you, and that the police had arrested you."

"Really? How does anyone know me? I am sure I don't keep friends."

"Of course they don't know you," he said with an air

of sarcasm. "They actually said, *Michael, it is your friend, the black guy you always hang out with.*"

I didn't like the sound of it, that people would begin to regard me a certain way when I walked about town. They might be thinking that I had committed an offense. I am an African after all, and as such it is a norm that I will be judged first, on parameters that don't pertain to others, before being heard. I wondered what people would be thinking as the reason for which I had been arrested. Who knows, they might be thinking that I had drugs on me and therefore had been busted. I told Michael about this thing.

"Why does it bother you so? You are working yourself out over nothing, bro. Chill. "

"Now you are sounding like the professor."

"You mean your friend?"

"Yes. As a matter of fact, he was the one who came to have me bailed at the station."

"Is that so?"

"Yea, and I regret causing him all that trouble. I had borrowed his access card, but I didn't know that it was an offense to use it at the Weston Library."

Michael sniggered. "So it was simply because you used another person's access card that these people called the police on you? And one would think they were accosting a terrorist who was out to blow up the place."

"It is really shocking."

"These people are really funny. And I was thinking

you had actually committed an offence or that they were mistaking you for another person."

"No. I just told you as it happened."

Michael laughed, and as though to prove how much inconsequential he considered it all to be, he began to talk about Annabelle and her friends and their planned trip to Turkey.

"I won't be going with you guys."

"And why is that?"

"I won't be able to afford the trip."

"And who told you that you are paying?"

"What do you mean by that? I don't understand you."

"I am paying for you. So don't worry."

"No, bro. I am afraid I won't allow it. I will have to decline."

But Michael would not have it. He drew close to me. "Listen here, my friend. There is this thing which you should understand about life. You see, the moment, you die, everything is finished for you. And this thing called death doesn't give any warning before it happens. So you should live life to the fullest when you have the opportunity. Come to think of it, was it not you who was just arrested? Imagine for instance that you were imprisoned. You would just lose your freedom just like that in a twinkle of an eye, and nobody would be able to help you. Not even your Nigerian professor friend."

"But I am not imprisoned."

"My point exactly! I am glad you are getting it. Now that you are not imprisoned, live life in celebration of freedom. Live life in thanksgiving. It is an act worship to God who has secured life and freedom for you."

"You are saying all of these to convince me to allow you lavish money on this holiday trip for me."

"Not for you, my brother. It is for me. How do you expect I handle all three girls on that trip? It would be too much of a burden for me looking out for them and making sure that no one is bored. But with you as my buddy, we can all share in the fun and responsibility as we have always been doing. I want you there, bro. I really do."

"Michael …"

"Please don't say anything before you pass a death sentence on me, bro. I can't have you put me in a situation where I would have to explain your absence at this vacation. Just think about my offer. I will be buying our tickets this weekend."

"It's the good heart of the toad that made him foolish."

TWENTY-EIGHT

Kabrit plizyè mèt mouri nan solèy

A goat that has several masters, will starve in the sun.

Mr. Klaus had been to prison once.

There was no information as to the reason for it.

But if I could hazard a guess, I would say that his offence might be racially motivated and that he had not repented of it one bit.

While in Father Anthony's house I had read about Adolf Hitler and the Nazi party in Germany and all that was done to the Jews in Europe, and on more than one occasion I had had the privilege of discussing the subject with Father Anthony as it was a topic I soon found him to be passionate about.

With Mr. Klaus and his goons taking over, the poultry farm and the house were no longer as I had known it to be, and many times I found myself wishing that the accident had never happened to Monsieur Benoit and that they had not had to sell off his property to the lot who now occupied and ran it. At that point I felt I could do anything to reverse what had happened. Even the displeasure of Madame Julia felt bearable as compared to what I daily had to put up with.

As for Mr. Wolfgang, he hardly showed up at the place but the first time he had come, he had told me what I was to be paid weekly. Two hundred euros. I didn't know what that sum amounted to or what it could do for me. It was the first time that I would be having some monetary value attributed to my labours. Yet something in me told me to contest it and I did. I told Mr. Wolfgang that my proposed wage was nothing short of a pittance, to which he treated me with a stare that told of his disbelief - I couldn't tell whether his disbelief was for my temerity to ask for a better salary or for something else.

"Boy," he addressed me in his accent that sounded strange and harsh to my ears. "You will never find anything better than what I have offered you."

And with that I knew that any further attempts at negotiations were out of the question. Clearly I could tell that I would be dealing with a man who was decisive in things involving money and negotiations and this made me wonder if Monsieur Benoit had gotten a fair deal for his property.

A part of me doubted it. Mr. Wolfgang and his stooges didn't elicit that kind of confidence and I told myself then that it would serve me better if I had plans for myself. I decided then that I would save every bit of my wages and when I could afford it, I would move to Paris, away from the poultry farm and Mr. Wolfgang and his stooges. Returning to the orphanage was out of the question.

I would take my chances in the world rather than remain at the mercy of people for when they needed me and when they tired of me.

Already it had become to look like all of my life everyone tired of me at some point. Haiti had tired of me and had sent me off to an orphanage in faraway France.

At the orphanage, I had become tiresome and had been carted away to Father Anthony's house who then, with the arrival of the mysterious visitor, had eventually seen for the burden that I was and returned me to the orphanage.

Why hadn't he taken me along with him wherever it was he was fleeing to overseas? Of course, the answer remained that I was an inconvenience, and so he had returned me, just as he had carted me away, to orphanage; a place which had grown to have no desire to keep me within its walls and had not wasted any time to ship me off with Mr. Benoit whilst clearly telling me that I was not welcome back should ever my foster home decided to tire of me.

And now with the accident, I still did not find any use for Mr. Benoit and his wife, wherever it was they were headed to when they had sold their property. Good a thing they had not returned me to the orphanage. And I was sure I wouldn't have let it for I had had my fill of being carted back and forth. I would have rebelled, run away even, done the unthinkable by stealing whatever I suspected to have any value; anything that could be pawned. Good a thing I had not been confronted with the option, for then it would still break my heart that I had treated Mr. Benoit so, because I would know that he would never have conceived of the idea had not his wife insisted on it, and if I had stolen to pay my way to some far off place and if the item stolen had it been something of immense importance to her, then all the better; it would please me so, and if ever I would lose a moment's sleep over it, it would be to laugh and congratulate myself. Yet all of these had not happened, and I was presented with an opportunity to plan and make my way in the world. I made up my mind to take it, to keep my head down, stay away from any confrontations with Mr. Klaus and his goons, and everything I did would be geared towards an expectation of my wages at the end of the week which ultimately would equip me for the move to Paris.

TWENTY-NINE

Sòt pa touye, men li fè ou swe

Stupidity doesn't kill, but it makes us sweat.

I remember that my father had always held a liking for books and people who read a lot, but somehow he wasn't the kind of people he admired.

He never had time for books and never read any. Many times when he talked about it, he had blamed his lack of reading on the demands of adulthood and parenting. He would talk about how much as a boy he used to read and spend time in the library, and when he talked about it, anyone could see his desire for his children to covet the habit of reading, yet he did little other than send us to school and purr over our school results for any hint of poor performance on our part. He rarely rewarded us when we excelled but he was sure to punish us when we performed badly in school. Sometimes he did it with a lash of his belt. But when the bad performance wasn't so severe, the offender could do away with some verbal threat.

When I thought about my friendship with Dr Chukwuemeka, it struck me that I could be making my father proud.

I imagined him knowing that I was friends with a renowned professor in Oxford of all places.

For even though my father had a high regard for professors, yet he never befriended any and hardly found himself in their circles, but whenever he did find himself amongst any who was lettered, his stance was attended with genuflections and posturing such as were reminiscent of idolatry.

He definitely would have marveled in the knowledge of the company I was keeping, and for this I felt pity for him; that he had been cut off in his prime so suddenly and didn't grow old enough to see how things were playing out. But what if the earthquake hadn't happened?

Would I have been in Oxford?

It was Dr Chukwuemeka that I told about how I came to be in Oxford.

He had actually asked to know.

I think my story was stretching too far and he was growing impatient to cut to the chase, so I told him how I had left Mr. Klaus and his goons behind and hitched many rides to Paris.

It didn't happen as peacefully as I had envisioned.

We had fought; myself and Mr. Klaus.

My relationship at the poultry farm was quite deteriorating as the weeks rolled into months. I began to pick certain words in German, not because of my interests in the language but these set of words were used too frequently whenever the speech was being directed at me that it didn't take long before I knew them to be curse words.

As they were frequently used, Mr. Klaus used those words. His goons did too. Yet I remained unperturbed setting my sights on the weekend when I would add my wage to the already growing pile in a box I had hidden in a hole somewhere in the farm. Even now I desist to mentioning the exact spot because I still feel that Mr. Klaus' goon could go dig it up and make a lot of my entire worldly goods.

On the morning that the fight happened I had let down a crate of egg and the whole thing had come crashing down to the floor. It must have been hunger or my growing anxiety, but my hands had shaken so badly, and I had dropped the crate.

Not one egg had survived the fall. And to my woes, misfortune had chosen that moment to bring Mr. Klaus in the farm even when his goons had been away at some party in the woods with some ladies the previous night and were yet to stir that morning. Mr. Klaus had noticed the accident, but he would not have it. He flew into a rage that got his face and scrawny neck all reddened like one of the layers that had reached the end of her term. He came over to me and went into a tirade of curses that made it appear like he was foaming in the mouth.

Much of his spit splattered on my face but I think he had picked offence when I stepped back to wipe his spit off my face. I was quick enough to dodge his swinging arm, but the fact that he had missed infuriated him the more. He unfastened his belt and bending it into a whip.

At that moment, I thought of home and what it felt like for my ancestors to be under the whip of the slave masters. My ancestors had revolted against it and toppled the reign of slavery, kicking the European slave dealers out of the island and investing in making other countries free from the shackles of slavery.

Yet here I was about to be treated as though I was not a descendant of those Africans who had defeated slavery and kicked the French out of Haiti. I didn't know where I had found the strength, but I lashed out at him with a kick to his knee and he buckled and cried out in pain.

Quickly I closed the gap between us and with all the anger that had held pent up for many months, I pounded him with my fist, never stopping until he stopped screaming lay still. It was when I rose to my feet that I saw all of his goons standing close by and spellbound. There was a certain fear in their eyes as they looked from my bloody wrist to their boss who lay limp and bloodied on the floor. They watched me turn around and leave, but they did not know that I had gone to my money stash and on to the house to pick up my already packed rucksack. Before they could get out of their shock, I was already gone.

I had hitched a truck of hay heading out of town and it was as the wind blew in my face as the truck sped along the countryside that I began to think that it was possible that I had killed a man.

THIRTY

Tout kòd gen de bout

"I am sure you didn't kill him," Dr. Chukwuemeka said.

"Yes, gratefully. I am glad I didn't although he had it coming for him," I said.

We were in his kitchen. I was helping out with chopping some onions while he tended to a pot of cattle leg with which he intended to make nkwobi. It would be the first time I would be tasting the food which he told me is a delicacy in Nigeria.

"So at what point did you realise that you had not murdered the German? What did you say his name was again? Mr …"

"Klaus. Mr Klaus."

"Yes, that is true. Mr Klaus. So at what point did you realise that you had not killed him?"

"Well, I have never known for sure. But if I had committed a murder … I mean it's been more than a while already … the French police would have been after me long before now."

"That is true."

"So how did you finally get to Oxford."

"When I got to Paris …" I began.

Paris was the beauty that I expected; the kind that seduced me and assured me that I had been right all along in my desire to see it. Yet it wasn't what I had expected. I got a room with the little money I had, but then there was this constant fear that I would soon run out of money and become like one of the people whom I saw sleeping in train stations or close to ATM machines. Paris looked to me to be one of those cold places where the iciness reached into people's hearts freezing up everything fluid and surging within it such that they crystallized into piercing stalagmites and stalactites. Paris! The city that had stood enchanting and alluring in the horizon of my vision didn't take long for its charm to begin to wear off and in its place was the constant fear that I could lose my mind.

Eventually my money ran out. It was a small sum after all, accumulated over four months yet it amounted to my entire material worth. The reality was such that I had dreaded, and which had spurred me upon a desperate search for jobs. Once I had chanced upon a store that appeared beat down and gave off such aura of neglect from a good distance, and in the hope that at least they would need a hand to give it some good cleaning, I had walked in. Nobody had answered my timid greetings or welcomed me at the counter. Determined, I went around the counter and because there was not much lighting about the place, I stumbled on something which I found out to my misfortune to be a sleeping pair.

"Who is that?!" one of them screamed in an accent which was something far removed from what I have ever heard from Europeans. A light bulb came on at that instant and I saw two men staring at me. The one who had screamed had a pistol in his hand, and his fellow stood quite ruffled, at the wall where a light switch was. In the fright that took hold of me then I took in the details of both men. They looked skinny with sunken cheekbones and disheveled hair the colour of corn silk that reached to their eyes and the nape of their necks. It was a surprise that I had not picked up their stench when I had walked through the door. On the floor where they had been roused from were sleeping bags and a few other things that suggested at personal effects, amongst them being two hypodermic needles and syringes and pieces of tubing.

"I am sorry … I …"

"Are you the police?" the one who had drawn out his gun asked, beginning to lower in remorsefully.

"No … No," I said. "I … I thought I could get a job here … I was just passing by."

At that moment I knew I had said the wrong thing for the gunman, emboldened, cocked the pistol and pointed it in my face.

"You have money?" he asked, rubbing his fingers in my face for emphasis. "Money?"

With my hands in the air, I confessed to him that I had no money and was simply a refugee looking for a job. But he would not have it. Tossing the gun aside, he and his partner swooped down on me. With a frenzy that was as wild as it was weird, they wrestled me to the floor and began to search through my pockets and every bit of my clothing. They felt around my collar, cuffs and the hem of my clothing. Their hands shook badly while they were at it. And then, they took off my shoes and would have ripped the entire thing about in their hope that there could be something of value I had stashed away within its sole or fabric. Distraught that they found nothing of value on me, they went into a fit of anger, kicking and yelling at anything within reach. One of them flung my shoe against the wall in frustration. In their state, they appeared to have forgotten all about me and realizing my chance I bolted for the door, never stopping until I was many metres away from the scene of a most indescribable madness - and without shoes on a cold Paris morning.

Dr Chukwuemeka laughed when I told him about my experience in Paris; how I had come to the *city of love* as I thought it to be and saw what for the people transcended love and romance; the importance paid to the basic instinct of individual and communal survival and how all of these was safely hidden away behind the facade of sophistication and popularity.

"I had lived in Paris when I was much younger," Professor Emeka said. "I had gone to Paris then as a young writer. I believed that no great artist of their day spent their entire lives without living in Paris for some time."

"Was it different in your day?"

"You mean Paris?"

"Yes."

He shrugged. "Will Paris ever change?"

"So you mean then that Paris is the same situation as it was in your day."

"I was too young then to realise that just like me, many other young and bright eyed artists with lofty dreams and expectations of the city had been drawn by its fame. But how was I to know, a young man from Nigeria, that long before my parents were born, many people had had their fair share of frustration and success in Paris. As for me, I was glad to leave Paris when I was able to. And I wasn't even prepared when I left. I left my bags and belonging in Paris, and it's been over two decades already."

"Really?"

"Yes. I think it has to do with the attitude of the French. They desire for you to be, as an African, everything they expect a second class Frenchman to be. They make things difficult for you when you don't speak their language and blend into every aspect of their identity while abandoning yours. It is some colonial policy that has to do with assimilation, as they say. Meanwhile they had spent the greater part of their civilization in plundering Africa, yet they put so much effort into staying ignorant of the indigenous cultures from where they sustain they sustain the economic base of their country."

"For how long you spent in Paris?"

"Two years," he said without thinking it through. "And I got out as soon as the opportunity came calling. And you? How did you get out of France?"

"A fire accident," I said.

Dr Chukwuemeka paused long enough to look at me all over, evidently in search of any visible scars or something of the sort that could give away the proof that I had once been through a fire accident.

"Tell me about it," he said.

Eight months had dragged on and I had stopped keeping track of time. For me, it appeared everything stood still while the world got by; and that I did; watching the world go by from my sleeping mat at an underground station.

Unable to sleep, I would watch the people of Paris as they came and went. It became quite easy to tell tourist and resident apart; the assured and the uncertain; the one who had it going and the one racing against time on slippery slopes. And there were many of the latter, for then I began to see the world as being a racecourse through verdant pastures and still waters with everyone running blindfolded along the tracks. That was how I saw the world and everyone in it. But for me, I perceived my lot to be quite different, condemned to the spectator stands and never to partake in a lot of others lest it be a foul play with a steep offense.

There were others like me who slept in their bags in the train station. I made friends with some but when they robbed me of some money and food without a care for recompense or what it would mean for the camaraderie we shared. It didn't take long for me to see that circumstances had cast my lot amongst such that cared for little else than the desire to live into the next day, at least. The only value they had for each other was the little sense of assurance that came with the feeling that each man wasn't alone in his misery, and that there were some others to look at and draw confidence or derive some laughter from. If the offer were to come, anyone would slit his neighbour's throat in their sleep and then return to their sleeping mat with the gladness that comes with having been paid. It didn't matter if the pay was in the form of money, food or drugs.

As long as something to ease life for a moment was offered, the job was certain to be done as expected.

Sometimes some of them took out his grouse on another while the rest cheered on enjoying the entertainment that the brawl offered.

We all lived boring and painful lives; the scum of the earth that the rest of the world would never want to see, and so whatever made us forget our lot for a moment was a welcome development.

Sometimes the police came to disturb us.

They would drive us away, but they would never hang around for more than a day and by then we would resume our places as though we never left.

In moments of introspection I was sure to direct certain questions at myself for like a compass to a sailor it was the one thing that kept me on course. But I was losing that desire for introspection. It had become for me the one thing that upset my spirit, sending it into such turbulence that got me feeling lost all the more.

And I hated the feeling.

It was better, I felt, to simply drift and take everything

as they came in good strides since it appeared that the more, I struggled against the tide, the more it appeared to me that I was sure to drown. Every morning, I would go into the city in the hope of something - anything at all that would keep me alive for the day. Long had I given up on the prospects of a job.

Nobody would employ me. I resorted to begging. It was the tourists that I targeted, the ones who looked like they came from Africa, for these were the ones I had learned to have a large heart. One of them had bothered to question me, and soon as he had learned a few things about me, he took me to get me a change of clothes even though the shop manager would have called the police to take my sorry sight away from his establishment. The tourist had bought me food in takeaway packs and gave a hundred euro note before leaving me a path.

He said he was Nigerian, and I could see how he struggled with himself as he left apparently sorry that he could not do much more for me. It was not every day, though, that one met a tourist like the Nigerian, for sometimes one was met with so much response that reminded them of the nuisance that they had become to society. Whatever one did with such responses, society wouldn't care.

It was up to the person whether to think of bailing out on life or thinking about becoming once again a part of society.

I think my chance came one day, when famished and met with no success in soliciting for alms, I had made my way to a fine neighbourhood.

It was my intention that I would rummage through their refuse bins for anything of value; food or anything that I could trade for something else. This was a neighbourhood that had those special bins where people deposited their used clothing and belongings for some charitable organisations in Africa, not knowing that these clothes ended up in markets in Africa. It was the second time I was going to that neighbourhood. The first time a resident had spotted me in their bins as I foraged, and when I had seen a police car approach, I had fled.

So this time, it was different. The neighbourhood was not the quiet one I had known all this time. People were crowded around a building on fire. Everyone had vacated. But a woman in the crowd was hysterical as her toddler was still on the fourth floor. Everyone was talking at once and pointing to the burning building. They said a gas leak had happened and the fire had begun with an explosion. The fire service had been notified and were yet to arrive.

No one noticed me in the crowd, a homeless kind, the type which they will never want to have amongst them, and if they did notice me, they didn't register it.

At that point of communal desperation no one cared

about much that didn't matter. And for me, I wasn't bothered either. The things that had bothered me about myself and my place in comparison with others didn't matter.

All what I was thinking about was the burning building and the toddler trapped in the apartment.

Maybe if I had thought about it, I would not have done it. But I sprinted towards the building and in a moment I had scaled the wall and was up on a balcony of the first floor.

Perching precariously on the railing, I leaped onto the next floor, and repeating the process I got onto the fourth floor and climbed into the apartment that was already becoming engulfed with smoke that made it difficult to see around the apartment. Quite alright, I could hear the wails of the toddler.

Without wasting a moment, I charged into the burning house using the cries of the baby as a guide until I came to a door.

Quite alright, the toddler was in her play pen in a room where for the sake of the closet door, the fire and smoke had not gotten to.

Upon seeing me, the toddler had stopped crying and stretched her arms to me. Instinctively I swept the toddler up in my arms and looking around the room, my eyes settled on a bed. I snatched off the blanket, wrapped the baby in it and charged out towards the balcony even as the fire began to rage amidst the sounds of fire truck sirens approaching from the distance.

It was when I had descended with the toddler, secured with the bedsheets the same way that my mother used to carry babies on her back while she went about her business of the day, that I heard the cheerful laughter, catcalls and praised from the crowd.

Hands received me, patted me and hugged me, and tears came to my eyes even as my limbs shook with fright and my mind began to register the risk I had thoughtlessly taken with my life.

"So that was how you came to be in Oxford? Through a scholarship?" Dr Chukwuemeka asked.

"Yes. It was not as though the Giovanni family did not present me with other options, but I was done with France. I needed a fresh start, and because my father always thought highly of Oxford, it was the first place that came to mind when I was asked what I desired in place of the offers that I was turning down. I am glad that I chose it because even though the bursary I receive isn't generous, yet it would see me through school."

"To be able to afford you a place here, your benefactors must be generous."

"The Giovanni might not be happy with their daughter's choice of a marriage partner and moving over to France in rebellion, but they were willing to offer so many choices as reward to the man who saved the life of their grandchild."

"Italians?"

"Yes."

"Now, I am curious," Dr. Chukwuemeka said, sweeping aside a stray lock of hair. "What offers did they present you with?"

"Training as a firefighter, a stipend, citizenship, many other things."

"So why didn't you choose to be a firefighter? Why did you turn down other opportunities and choose to come this way instead?"

"As a destitute I had taken the time to observe society and so when I was presented with a blank cheque, I chose the one option that would take me to the top of society and secure my place there rather than settle for being a celebrated working class member of a harsh society."

"I think that makes a lot of sense," he said thoughtfully.

"Besides, it would please my father more were he to know that I am a student at University of Oxford."

"He would be scared if he were to see you earning this opportunity. And by the way, that was a brave thing you did saving that baby."

"Thank you. I am glad you think that of me."

"Don't get ahead of yourself, my friend. And don't

let this get into you head so you don't start jumping into fires."

"I won't. I promise," I said laughing.

Dr. Chukwuemeka reached over and patted my shoulder, and then grunting, he rose to his feet.

"Have you heard of the proposed move to transfer asylum seekers in the UK to Rwanda?"

"Yes," I said. "I heard about it in the news."

"And what's your opinion?"

"I feel that it is because the UK wants to make room for Ukrainian refugees whom they consider to be more European and akin to them that every other second and third world nationals seeking asylum. I mean, they don't bother to conceal the fact that they have no problems accommodating Ukrainian refugees because they are fellow Europeans. And I also believe that once asylum seekers are shipped off to Rwanda, I mean for an African, that is deportation already."

"There will be a lecture at the Weston Library next week. It is on this issue. Since you like coming to listen to lectures, you will find this one interesting."

I scratched my head, and at that moment, began to reconsider my decision to go with Michael and the ladies on the vacation in Turkey.

"But don't worry," he added. "I won't be giving you my access card this time."

I laughed.

He added, "Every rope has two ends."

Epilòg

Well, the lion spirit of the deep and rich and curious continent, I am once again living on the edge, which may be exciting in some ways, as thrilling as Shakyamuni Buddha under his Bodhi tree, hungry for enlightenment and willing to sit there until the internal processes lined up like striations in an Amethyst crystal, each layer an organic settling of inherent qualities.

I have been sitting under the second of three oak trees in a park of green lawn vistas and feeling the joy of a thousand suns bursting into some kind of radiant awareness of self-effulgence.

The circle is nearly complete and one pointed focus of the ebullient mind is almost ready to burn laser holes in the stony delusion that has many humans in it's eerie thrall.

Truth is, always a good thing to use as a waxed board on a curling wave of phenomena, impermanent as it usually is.

Bodhisattva, Satguru, Avatara, Rasul, Kalachakra.

Scintillating are the ways and flavours of the beings who come when needed, angels and sisters of mercy unbound.

I am working on a crappy little notebook, skipping cursor is the anti-Christ at the moment, but even this can be transformed into gold sparkles with a knowing laugh.

We should really find a way to connect, so much more fluid and dialogue friendly.

I would love many long conversations with you, the mind in your oceans, the spark in your tinderbox and tell the world all about Haiti, where they can enjoy Makawoni au graten, Bouillon Soup, tchaka, legim, tassot, patty, pikliz, joumou, griot, Poulet aux noix, Bouillie de Bananes Plantains, Diri ak Lalo, Pain Patate, TomTom ak Kalalou Gombo, Bouillon tèt kabrit, Diri Djondjon, Bonbon Siwo, Akasan, Dous Makòs, Kasav, and other kinds of stuff.

The beauty of Haiti has eluded the world.

Acknowledgements

This book was inspired by true event. Thank you, Dudley O'Shaughnessy, for always bringing sunshine. Grateful to Ikenna Okeh, who was instrumental in shaping up this narrative and making it look real.

My dear friend, Obiora Anozie, whose support is unwavering. And Aneto Emeka Chukwuka. Thank you so much.

I want to thank: Professor Wale Adebanwi, Professor David Pratten, Professor Miles Larmer and Professor James Currey. They made it possible for me to join the African Studies Centre.

Much thanks to Alexandra Franklin and Lucy Bayley, of Bodleian Libraries. For everything.

Eternal gratitude to Juliet Mabey of OneWorld Publications.

Ebuka Iloegbunam, Mishael Maro Amos, Bobby Onyeocha, Lanre David Messan, Emmanuel Ikechukwu Umeonyirioha, Kelvin Kellman, Hymar David, Mitterand Okorie, Chike Odigie, Chinedu Ohiaeri, Nky Iweka, Kargbo Bockarie and Samson Onwe. Thank you all!

My manager, Debbie Edwards. Motherly soul. Thank you! Pelagie Okorie and Salma Idris, thank you!

My partner in India, Dinesh Chakravarthy. I appreciate you.

Stephen Embleton, at Abibiman Publishing and the Anne Nwakalor, for everything!

I am thankful to my parents, Sam and Ona, who have always supported me.

My siblings, Chijioke, Odinaka, Nkechi, Ebere and Ifeanyi – I appreciate you!

Grateful to Rasaq Malik Gbolahan and Ebelenna Tobenna Esomnofu, for editing. Bless you. And thanks also, to Ifeanyi Mojekwu at Abibiman Publishing.

I appreciate my people in Haiti: Jean-Claude Dorsainvil and Mikerson Payant, who made all the corrections in Creole.

Ever Obi - my beautiful kind friend. For being. And Ifeoma Ifeanyi-Odinye. For the support. Much appreciated.

For all the support, thanks to former Foreign Affairs Minister of Haiti, Dr. Claude Joseph, who accepted my invitation to come speak at Weston Library and the Ambassador of Haiti to the United Kingdom, H.E.M Euvrant Saint Amand.

Thanks to Merline Ulysee, who introduced me to Professor Dorleans Henri, who said to me: "Come to Haiti, without your wallet. You have a home here!"

Mèsi.

Lightning Source UK Ltd.
Milton Keynes UK
UKHW040352260822
407828UK00013B/418